The Lady from Nowhere
A Detective Story

Fergus Hume

The Lady from Nowhere: A Detective Story

Copyright © 2024 Indo-European Publishing

The present edition is a reproduction of previous publication of this classic work. Minor typographical errors may have been corrected without note; however, for an authentic reading experience the spelling, punctuation, and capitalization have been retained from the original text.

ISBN: 979-8-88942-490-1

CONTENTS

Chapter I	The Tragedy of the Strange Room	1
Chapter II	The Death-card	7
Chapter III	A Woman without a Past	14
Chapter IV	The Five Landladies	20
Chapter V	A Friend in Need	25
Chapter VI	The Crime of Kirkstone Hall	30
Chapter VII	Comments on the Crime	36
Chapter VIII	Mr. Prain, Solicitor	42
Chapter IX	Kirkstone Hall	48
Chapter X	Strange Behaviour	53
Chapter XI	The Mad Gardener	58
Chapter XII	The Diamond Necklace	64
Chapter XIII	Arthur Ferris	70
Chapter XIV	A Surprising Discovery	76
Chapter XV	The Revelation of Mr. Prain	81
Chapter XVI	Miss Wedderburn	87
Chapter XVII	An Explanation	92
Chapter XVIII	What Mrs. Presk found	98
Chapter XIX	The Unexpected occurs	104
Chapter XX	A Needle in a Haystack	109
Chapter XXI	Found at Last	115
Chapter XXII	A Secret Hoard	120
Chapter XXIII	The Convict's Defence	125
Chapter XXIV	Proof Positive	131
Chapter XXV	How the Deed was done	137
Chapter XXVI	The End of it All	144

CHAPTER I

THE TRAGEDY OF THE STRANGE ROOM

On the night of July 24th, in the year 1896, between the hours of eleven and twelve, Grangebury, a little-known suburb of London, was wrapped in slumber, as became a respectable neighbourhood whose inhabitants retired regularly shortly after sunset. Not that they had done so on this particular night, for the unusual excitement of a lecture on Dickens, delivered in the tiny Town Hall, had kept them from their beds later than was customary. At a quarter to eleven, a stream of instructed pleasure-seekers, discussing lecture and lecturer, filled the narrow streets; but gradually the crowd diminished until highways and byways were left deserted, save by watchful policemen and vagrant cats. The lamps were then extinguished by order of an economical municipality, the few lights still twinkling from the upper windows of various houses disappeared, and the little town lay under moon and stars as silent and almost as lonely as the spell-bound cities in eastern fables.

Every now and then the footsteps of policemen making their rounds, could be heard echoing along the streets, and sometimes an official lantern would be flashed into dark corners to search out possible burglars or homeless beggars. But no thieves or vagabonds could be discovered; for, on the whole, Grangebury, being a comparatively new suburb, was free from such criminal pests, and the police force there, under the command of Mr. Inspector Lackland had a very easy time. There was nothing on this night to indicate any ending to this Arcadian Age of security and innocence; yet, shortly after eleven o'clock a yawning policeman, leaning against a convenient wall, heard a word cried aloud which told him of crime and danger. The word was "Murder!"

"Murder!" repeated the constable, looking up and down the street.

"Murder!" shrieked the voice again; and then there came the sound of running feet, cries for help, and the quick panting of an exhausted creature. Before the policeman could decide in which direction to move, a dishevelled woman, screaming and gesticulating, came at full speed round the corner, and almost fell into his arms. Her face was pearly white in the moonlight, her eyes were filled with terror, and an almost continuous cry issued from her open mouth without any motion of the lips.

"'Ere! 'ere, wot's this?" said the policeman, seizing the flying creature by the arm. "Wot d'ye mean, screeching out murder like a loonatic? Come now!"

Trembling violently, the woman grappled with the policeman, shrieking the while, and evidently beside herself with terror. Not being gifted with brains, the officer of the law shook her vigorously to brighten her intellect; and she wavered limply in his grasp like a dummy figure.

"Murder!" she whimpered, clawing and clutching at the man. "Lord! it's awful! Ugh! Ugh! I've seen her dead!"

"Seen 'oo dead?" demanded the policeman, stolidly.

"My lodger! Dead! Strangled! Ugh! Ugh!" cried the woman, breathlessly, raising her voice higher at each word. "A corpse in the Yellow Room! Paradise Row! Come and see—come and—— Oh, poor soul!" and she fell to wringing her hands again, quivering and panting.

"Wait a bit!" said the jack-in-office, bound by red-tapeism, "the police station is just roun' th' corner. Kim up an' see th' Inspector!"

"I—I—I am innocent!" gasped the woman, hanging back. "Neither 'Tilda nor I laid a finger on her."

"'Oo said y' did?" retorted the man, suspiciously; and, for his own protection he recited an official formula, "Wot y' say now 'ull be used in hevidence agin y'. Kim up, I tell y'." And, grasping her arm, he hurried her fighting and crying round the near corner, and into a red-brick building, over the door of which was a lamp inscribed "Police Station."

In a stuffy room, rendered almost unbearable by the heat of the flaring gas, two men were talking earnestly together, notwithstanding the lateness of the hour. The one in uniform was a burly, red-faced martinet known in Grangebury as Inspector Lackland. He was too completely hemmed in by red tapeism to count for much; but the other in plain clothes was Absolom Gebb, well known in Scotland Yard as a capable detective, but not so infallible as the miracle-monger of fiction. It was Gebb who brought home the theft of Lady Daleshire's diamonds to herself; who proved Dr. Marner to be guilty of poisoning his wife, in spite of strong evidence to the contrary; who solved nine out of every ten criminal problems submitted to him, and who was the terror of all evil-doers. This tall, lean man with his clean-shaven face and black, observant eyes was an enthusiast in his profession, and loved to ponder over and follow out the intricacies of criminal mysteries. At the present moment he was conversing with Lackland about a recent Anarchist conspiracy, and therefore happened to be in the Grangebury Police Office when the zealous policeman appeared with his terrified

2

prisoner. She cried out when she was thrust into the room, and, confronted by inspector and detective, covered her face with her hands.

"Hey! What!" said Lackland, in his rasping voice. "What's all this about?"

"Case of murder, sir," jerked out the policeman, pushing forward the prisoner. "Paradise Row! Woman strangled!"

"Murder?" cried Gebb, pricking up his ears at the ominous word.

"Murder!" screeched the woman, and fell into a chair. Evidently she had received a shock and was on the verge of hysterics, for she began to babble and weep copiously. Accustomed to deal with this sort of emotion, Lackland seized a jug of water standing near his desk, and dashed the contents into her face. The remedy was efficacious, for with a gasp and a shiver the woman recovered her self-control and tongue, also her inherent feminine vanity. "You brute!" she screamed, jumping up wrathfully. "My best bonnet's spoilt."

"Attention!" roared the inspector in his sternest military manner; "none of this nonsense here. What about this murder in—"

"I didn't kill her!" interrupted the woman, wiping her face. "'Tilda and me knew nothing about it till we found her strangled when we came back from the lecture."

"Did you attend the lecture on Dickens in the Town Hall?" asked Gebb.

"Yes, I did, sir; both me and 'Tilda, who is my servant, went."

"What is your name?" asked the detective, with professional sharpness.

"Maria Presk."

"Married or single?"

"Married once, single now," sighed the woman. "I am what you call a widow, sir; and I let lodgings in Paradise Row."

"Was this dead woman a lodger of yours?"

"Miss Ligram, you mean? Yes. Miss Ligram was in the first floor front."

"And who killed Miss Ligram?" asked Gebb, looking keenly at Mrs. Presk.

The good lady turned ever paler than before.

"I—I don't know, sir," she stammered, with a scared look. "I can take my stand in any court of——"

"Face this way, ma'am!" interrupted Lackland, who was indignant at the way in which Gebb was usurping his authority. "I'm in charge of this office. I'm the officer to take your evidence. Mr. Gebb! Discipline!"

3

"Alright! Go ahead!" replied the detective, inwardly cursing the too methodical procedure of his superior, "I don't want to interfere. But," he added with emphasis, "I think we should go at once and look at the corpse."

"All in good time, Mr. Gebb. More haste, less speed!" said Lackland, crisply.

"And the more delay, the less chance of getting at the truth," retorted Gebb.

The fact was that Gebb's sporting instincts were roused, and he wanted to be off on the trail while it was yet fresh. Every moment was of importance. Yet, as he was not in charge of the case, he was forced to stand idly by and hear the blundering inspector putting a lot of irrelevant questions—good for nothing, but wasting time. However, Gebb managed to extract some grains of wheat out of a vast quantity of chaff, and in a roundabout way—thanks to the inspector's method of questioning—learned the following facts, which were sufficient to inform him how matters stood at present.

Miss Ligram was—or rather, had been, since she no longer existed—a lodger in the house of Mrs. Presk, No. 13, Paradise Row. She was a quiet, inoffensive old lady, who gave little trouble, and who remained by preference in her own room. On the night of the 24th July, Mrs. Presk and her servant, Matilda Crane, had attended a lecture delivered in the Town Hall. The lecture—an amusing one on Charles Dickens and his works—had afforded them much pleasure, and they returned at eleven o'clock to Paradise Row in a state of high spirits. On passing round to the back entrance they saw that a light was still burning in Miss Ligram's sitting-room, and, wondering at the sight—for the lodger usually retired early—Mrs. Presk, on entering the house, had gone upstairs to see if anything was wrong. To her horror she found Miss Ligram dead, with a cord round her neck. Terrified by the sight, she had called up Matilda Crane, who, more impressionable and less hardened, had promptly fainted away. Mrs. Presk, a woman of energy and resource, had immediately sought the aid of the police, and now insisted that Lackland and his subordinates should remove the corpse and capture the murderer.

"That last is easier said than done," was Gebb's comment on this demand. "By this time the assassin is far enough away. However, there's no time to be lost in looking at the scene of the crime, as I suggested."

"Quite so," said Lackland, gruffly. "No time to waste, ma'am"—to Mrs. Presk. "March! Gebb, come with me and catch the murderer!"

This proposition recommending itself to Mrs. Presk, she left the police-office with inspector and detective, and led the pair to her house, which was situated down a side street no great distance away. As the front door was closed, she conducted the men round the back way, through the kitchen, and up the stairs into Miss Ligram's sitting-room. On the mat in the passage, 'Tilda, the servant, lay still insensible, so Mrs. Presk lifted her in her strong arms and carried her to the kitchen to be revived as speedily as possible, in case, as was almost certain, her evidence might be wanted. In the mean time Lackland and Gebb had entered the room wherein the crime had been committed, and were amazed at the splendour of the apartment. For colouring and evidence of wealth it was like a scene out of the Arabian Nights.

The room was of no great size, with a window looking out on to the street, and two doors, one leading in from a narrow passage, the other giving admittance into an inner apartment, evidently a bedroom. The walls were draped with rich hangings of satin, yellow as a buttercup in hue, and a tent-like roof of the same tint and material was drawn in many folds to a dome-like centre, whence depended by a brass chain an Arabian lantern studded with knobs of yellow glass, which, illuminated from within, shone like pale topaz stones. Tables, chairs, and couches were framed of gilded cane, with coverlets and quilts of yellow silk, and the ground of the carpet was of the same colour, embroidered with bunches of primrose flowers. Also there were tall narrow mirrors framed in yellow satin, clusters of daffodils in grotesque Chinese vases of a deep yellow shade, and numerous candles—all lighted—in candelabra silver gilt. Near the window, from a brass chafing-dish standing on a tripod of the same metal, curled up a thin white vapour diffusing a heavy rich perfume, and everywhere lay nicknacks of gold and silver more or less costly; fur mats and rugs dyed yellow, and many books covered in a homely fashion with yellow paper. The prevailing colour of the room was a violent yellow; and this, with the glare of the candles, the glitter of the mirrors, the scent of the flowers, and the strong perfume of the incense, made the heads of the onlookers reel. Even the matter-of-fact inspector was impressed by the uncanny magnificence of the place.

"By George, sir!" said he to Gebb, with the instincts of an old soldier, "it's like a Mandalay Pagoda. If t'was in Burmah, now, shouldn't mind looting it."

Gebb was rubbing his hands, with sparkling eyes.

"By the sight of it," he said joyfully, "this is going to be a romantic case. I only hope I'll be lucky enough to get charge of it. Did you furnish this room, ma'am?" he asked, turning sharply to

5

Mrs. Presk, whose pale grey face appeared over the shoulder of the burly, staring inspector.

"No, I didn't," retorted the landlady. "Miss Ligram furnished it herself, and called it her Yellow Boudoir."

CHAPTER II

THE DEATH-CARD

If the appearance of the room was amazing, that of the dead woman was not less so. The body was lying loosely in an armchair, with sprawling legs and arms, like a saw-dust doll. The head lay limply on the shoulder, and a yellow cord—evidently torn from a near curtain—was bound tightly round the lean throat The distorted face, the protruding tongue, the bulging eyes, and discoloured skin, all showed that the poor creature had been strangled in the most remorseless manner. Before her was placed a low cane table, on the yellow coverlet of which a pack of cards was spread out face downward, but in the lap of the dead woman lay another card with the face upward. It was the ace of spades. Mrs. Presk noting it for the first time gave a screech of mingled horror and surprise.

"The death-card!" she gasped, stepping back. "Lord! how awful!"

"What do you mean by the death-card?" asked Gebb, sharply.

"Why!" said Mrs. Presk, astonished at the question, which to her seemed unnecessary, "it's the card in the pack as stands for death. When you turn up the ace of spades you know it's time to order your coffin."

"Rubbish!" said Gebb. "Humbug!" roared the inspector; and they both shrugged their shoulders to show their contempt for such superstition.

Mrs. Presk shook her head gloomily. "Talk won't alter the matter!" she said, pointing to the card. "There's the death-token, and there's the corpse; what do you make of that?"

"I make this," said Gebb, dryly; "that the murderer must be a person of imagination."

"He ought to be shot, the blackguard," growled Lackland, "play-acting with a corpse. I wonder what they were fooling with cards for? Looks like a madman's work to me. What do you say, Gebb?"

Gebb said nothing at the moment. He was examining the dead woman, who was arrayed with unusual splendour quite in keeping with the room, yet too richly for the front parlour of a fifth-rate lodging-house.

Miss Ligram's body was that of an old woman close upon sixty years of age, with a wrinkled face, and a profusion of silvery white

7

hair turned back in the style of Marie Antoinette. It was dressed in an old-fashioned dinner-dress of white silk, trimmed with valuable lace, and this was designed so as to show the lean neck and bony arms of the wearer. Anything more incongruous than that poor clay clothed in such costly garments can scarcely be imagined. It seemed to accentuate the grimness of the crime, almost to elevate a sordid murder to the level of tragedy.

"Did Miss Ligram usually dress like this?" asked Gebb, turning to Mrs. Presk.

"Every evening!" replied the landlady, promptly.

"She must have been eccentric!" was Gebb's comment on this reply.

"Very eccentric, sir. I don't think she was quite right here." And the landlady tapped her head significantly.

"A Crazy Jane?" questioned Lackland.

"She was and she wasn't," answered Mrs. Presk, enigmatically. "She wasn't mad enough to be shut up, but she acted in a queerer way than most people. Look at this room, and all its lights; every night it was the same. She usually dined off a chop and potatoes, yet she dressed in silk and lace to eat them. And——" Thus far Mrs. Presk with her eyes on the corpse had proceeded volubly, when suddenly—still staring at the dead woman—she stopped, and her jaw dropped. Motionless as a stone image she stood looking; and then with an ejaculation she ran out of the room. The detective and the inspector looked at her vanishing form, looked at the corpse, looked at one another, and failed to understand her action.

"What the devil does that mean?" said Gebb, with surly amazement.

"Only the devil knows," retorted Lackland, grimly; "but if that jade is hiding anything of importance the sooner we get it out of her the better. You're a bit of a lawyer, Gebb, so I'll bring back Mrs. Presk, and you'll examine her!"

"No!" said Gebb, detaining his friend; "let her go now. I'll get the truth out of her to-morrow."

"By George you will, will you!" grumbled Lackland, annoyed that his advice was not taken; "and what if you don't get charge of the case?"

"I'll grin and bear it, I suppose!" retorted the other; "but I'll work my hardest to be given the handling of this affair, for it strikes me that it will prove a sight more difficult than either of us guesses. This room's a rum one, ain't it? And that pack of cards aren't there for nothing. Then there is the dead woman's dress, and the landlady's queer conduct. Oh, you can bet, inspector, there's a jolly

8

lot more in these things than meets the eye, and I'm the man to find out what they all mean."

"You can blow your own trumpet, I see!" said Lackland, dryly.

Gebb laughed, in nowise embarrassed. "My trumpeter's dead from over-work," he replied coolly. "If I don't praise myself no one else will. However, I'll see to-morrow if the big wigs will let me run this show in my own way. Now you go and look round the house, Lackland, and leave me here to examine the room."

"What about the body?" asked the inspector, dominated by Gebb's strong will.

"We'll let it lie here as it is, until the doctor comes. I told that policeman who brought Mrs. Presk to the station to knock up an M.D."

"By George, sir, one would think you were inspector here!" spluttered the indignant Lackland. "Am I nobody?"

"You're a good fellow—too good to get your monkey up for nothing. You let me look after this murder myself. I'll do you a good turn some other time."

"Well, I'll let you have your own way for once. You're no fool, I will say," muttered Lackland, and withdrew to look through the house. He knew that Gebb was very clever, and in his heart was not unwilling to avail himself of the detective's assistance. Therefore, he left him to his own devices, and set out to seek Mrs. Presk in the kitchen. Having found her, he made her show him the house, but judiciously refrained from commenting on her late conduct. He left the elucidation of that to Gebb.

Left to himself, the detective examined the dead woman and the room with minute attention to detail, keeping up a running commentary the while on his discoveries. He had a habit of talking aloud when alone, as if to emphasize his opinions, and, while examining the boudoir, soliloquized with appropriate actions like a stage-player.

"The furniture is quite in order," he murmured, his keen eyes roving hither and thither. "Therefore there can have been no struggle. The murderer was no intruder, but was expected. A visitor! perhaps a friend! He—let me presume the criminal to be a man—he no doubt entered, and was kindly received by the deceased. Here is a bottle, and two glasses with wine in each; so the two were friendly enough to drink in company. There is a chair on either side of this table whereon the cards are laid out The dead body remains in the one nearest the wall; so I expect the visitor sat in the other with his back to the door. Were they playing cards? I think not, as in that case the whole pack would not be laid out in this fashion. I have it!" cried Gebb, smiting his open palm with his fist, "the visitor was

9

telling Miss Ligram's fortune. He placed the cards in that position and told her to draw one. She drew the ace of spades, which yet lies in her lap, and when face to face with the omen of death he killed her."

Here the detective paused to consider if he was correct in assuming the assassin to be a man. Fortune-telling—especially by cards—is usually indulged in by the other sex. But would a woman, however cruel, have so brutally strangled her unsuspecting hostess, and—as it may be assumed—friend? Gebb examined the chair on which the visitor had sat, and found traces of tobacco ash.

"Cigarette ash?" he pronounced it after an examination, "the quality is fine and quantity small. The visitor was a man and he was smoking. H'm! That is not like a professional fortune-teller. Such a one would be too desirous of impressing his dupe to spoil the gravity of the situation by smoking. The man must have been a friend, and he probably told the woman's fortune in this way to throw her off her guard. Let us look further."

The chair in which the dead body was lying, stood some little distance from the hangings of the wall. These, as Gebb discovered on further examination, had been draped back with a cord to reveal a small oil painting; but the cord—which had a loop at either end to slip over a brass nail, concealed beneath the hangings of satin—had been deftly removed (not torn) from its peg, and flung round the victim's neck. On the floor behind the chair Gebb picked up a half-burnt cigarette, which had smouldered out. With this in his hand he returned to the centre of the room and looked once more at the cards. These attracted him strangely.

"Without doubt the fortune-telling was a trick," he said aloud. "The man set out the cards, and while his victim was selecting one he lighted a cigarette, and rose to stroll round the room. Not suspecting any danger—which shows, by the way, that she must have trusted him—his victim let him pass behind her chair. While there, he slipped the loops of the cord off the nail. Then when she turned up the death-card—a pure coincidence, no doubt—he threw the cord over her head and choked her before the poor wretch had time to call out for assistance. He then robbed the body at his leisure, and left the house. It's as clear as day."

Presuming that the murderer had gone out by the front door, Gebb left the room and went into the passage. To his surprise he found that the front door was locked, but, as the detective noted, not bolted.

"He must have locked it after he left the house," thought Gebb, "and no doubt did so to prevent intrusion and a too sudden

10

discovery of his crime. I expect he threw away the key when outside. In the front garden most probably; I'll look."

Before he could put his design into execution, which he intended doing by passing out the back way, Mrs. Presk arrived downstairs with the intelligence that Inspector Lackland was still searching the upper portion of the house for traces of the assassin, but could find nothing and no one. "So," said she, "I expect the wretch ran away after killing poor Miss Ligram."

"By the front door," Gebb informed her, "and he locked it after him."

"Did he?" said Mrs. Presk, with a stare; "now that's queer."

"Why?" asked the detective, sharply.

"Because Miss Ligram always kept the front door locked, and the key in her pocket. That was one of her queer ways which I never could abide."

Without a word Gebb returned to the Yellow Boudoir, and searched in the pocket of the dead woman. Sure enough he found therein a large key which Mrs. Presk immediately declared to be that of the front door. Gebb was puzzled, as this discovery upset much of his previous reasoning.

"In that case the man could not have cleared out by the front," he said, "as not having the key he could not lock the door after him. Let us see the back door; he may have escaped in that direction."

"The back door was locked," said Mrs. Presk, promptly. "I had the key in my pocket when I went to the lecture."

"Was the door locked when you returned?" asked Gebb, more puzzled than ever.

"Yes, sir, it was. I had no thought that anything was wrong until I came upstairs and saw the corpse; though, to be sure," added Mrs. Presk, suddenly, "I fancied it strange that the lights should be burning so late in Miss Ligram's boudoir. I saw them from the road, you know, Mr. Gebb; and the sight gave me a turn, I can tell you."

"He must have got out through a back window," murmured Gebb.

"Indeed, he didn't, sir. When I brought 'Tilda out of her faint in the kitchen I looked at all the windows in the basement; they are all bolted and barred proper. 'Tilda and me's both careful on account of burglars."

Gebb pinched his chin and shook his head in a perplexed manner; after which he walked to the window of the yellow room and examined it carefully. It was fastened by a snick, the position of which showed that the window was closed, and could not have been used as an exit.

"Let alone the danger of the cove being seen by a chance

11

policeman, and taken up as a burglar," mused Gebb, "what about the upstairs windows, Mrs. Presk?"

"They're all locked, sir. Mr. Inspector examined every one."

"Then the man must be in the house still," was Gebb's final conclusion.

"He isn't," insisted Mrs. Presk, with a startled glance over her shoulder; "we've looked under all the beds, and into all the rooms and cupboards. Unless he is like a sparrow on the house-top, I don't know where he can be."

"Well, there doesn't seem any way by which he could get out," said Gebb, in a vexed tone. "Did you hear any sound in the house when you arrived home?"

"No, I didn't, sir. I went up to see if Miss Ligram was ill, as I noticed that her room was lighted up, then I saw the corpse, and called 'Tilda, who ran up and fainted. She ain't got my nerves, Mr. Gebb."

"Did you lock the back door when you came in?"

"Lawks, no, sir! 'Tilda and me was in such a flurry to see if Miss Ligram was ill that we just left the door anyhow.

"When you went upstairs was the door closed to?"

"I think so," replied Mrs. Presk, after a pause, "for 'Tilda banged it to; but it wasn't locked, I'll take my dying word on that."

"When you came for the police did you leave by that door?"

"Yes, I did; by the back door, as Miss Ligram kept the front one locked."

"Was it closed when you went out?"

Mrs. Presk looked up suddenly, rather alarmed. "No sir, it wasn't," said she in startled tones, "It was—as you might say—ajar."

"Aha!" said Gebb, triumphantly, "then you may depend upon it, Mrs. Presk, that when you came home the assassin was in the house."

"In the house!" gasped Mrs. Presk. "Lor, sir! it ain't possible."

"Yes! he did not know where to find the front-door key; and discovering that the back door was locked, he just hid himself in the kitchen until you and the servant went upstairs to look on his handiwork. Then he slipped out to escape the consequences."

Mrs. Presk's knees gave way, and she was fain to sit down—as far away from the dead body as possible however. "It's past believing," she moaned, rocking herself to and fro. "Lord! what an escape 'Tilda and me's had from being strangulated. Ugh!" she shuddered, "look at that poor soul, sir, ain't it enough to freeze your blood."

"Did it freeze yours, that you ran out of the room?" asked Gebb, hoping to take her unawares.

12

"No! a'wasn't that!" whispered Mrs. Presk, turning pale, "but I was afeard!"

"Of what?" asked the detective, rather puzzled.

"Of you, sir," was the unexpected reply.

"Indeed! then you know something about the matter?"

"Yes!" issued from the landlady's pale lips, "I—I noticed something."

"What did you notice?"

"I daren't tell you."

"You must!"

Mrs. Presk rose and hastily made for the door. Before she could reach it Gebb had placed his back against it. "You don't leave this room until I know what you are hiding."

"I'm hiding nothing!" burst out Mrs. Presk, "haven't you got eyes?" She pointed towards the dead woman. "Look!" she cried "Look!"

CHAPTER III

A WOMAN WITHOUT A PAST

As desired, Gebb looked at the gaily decked figure in the chair, and tried to find out what Mrs. Presk meant.

"Well, I'm looking," he said at length, "but I'm blest if I can see anything."

"Of course you can't!" cried the landlady, hysterically triumphant, "'cause they ain't there!"

"What aren't there?"

"The diamonds!"

"Diamonds!" repeated Gebb, with a start, as he noted that the dead woman wore no jewellery. "Had she diamonds?"

"I should think she had!" said Mrs. Presk, sitting down again. "Stars for her hair, rings, bracelets, and the loveliest necklace you ever saw—just like dewdrops with the sun on them. She wore her jewellery every night, and all to eat her chop. I saw them diamonds on her afore I went to the lecture."

"And when you came back they were gone."

"Every one of them," replied Mrs. Presk, defiantly, "and when I noticed it—for, to own up, Mr. Gebb, I didn't notice they were gone till I was here with you talking about her dress—but when I did notice, I ran out of the room 'cause I was a-feared you might say 'Tilda and I stole 'em."

"Nonsense! Why should I say that?"

"Oh, there ain't no tellings," said Mrs. Presk, with a toss of her head.

"Was that why you made all that howling?"

"Yes, it was, sir; and I ran out to the kitchen to ask 'Tilda if she had noticed if the diamonds were gone when we came in first; for I was that flurried I didn't look for 'em."

"And does 'Tilda say the diamonds were gone?"

"Yes! I dessay the murdering villain who killed the poor dear stole 'em. I wish I had the hanging of him."

"Oh, you may assist me to put the rope round his neck," said Gebb. "Well, Mrs. Presk, I'll come and see you to-morrow, and you must tell me all you know about this woman. In the mean time, I think I hear the doctor coming."

The detective's ears had not deceived him, for the approaching footsteps were those of the doctor. Escorted by the policeman who

14

had met Mrs. Presk, he entered in no very good humour at being knocked up at so late an hour. However, the looks of the corpse, and the appearance of the room both astonished and interested him; and he made his examination. It took only a few minutes for him to decide that the death had taken place shortly before or after ten o'clock, and must have been almost instantaneous. When the examination was concluded, Gebb and the inspector left the house in charge of the policeman, and returned to the station to make their report. While the prosaic Lackland set down the bare details of the case for the information of the authorities, Gebb mused over the events of the night, and pondered what was best to be done under the circumstances.

As yet he had gained no information from Mrs. Presk about her lodger, but intended to examine her on the morrow when she was somewhat recovered from the strain of the late events. In the mean time, Gebb fancied that the strange room, designed and furnished by the dead woman, might turn out a more important factor in the matter than at present appeared. Even if Mrs. Presk did prove to be ignorant of Miss Ligram's past—which was extremely unlikely—the strongly marked and eccentric taste of the lodger, as exemplified in illumination, colouring, and furnishing, might provide a sufficiently stable basis for operations. In a word, Gebb considered that the most promising clue to the mystery was the predominance of the colour yellow in the sitting-room. Criminal problems, as he knew, had been solved by slighter means.

As Lackland surmised, Gebb, being high in favour with the authorities as a detective of no ordinary capabilities, had little difficulty in gaining their consent to taking charge of the case. The inspector made his report, Gebb his application, and after the due formalities had been complied with, the detective found that the responsibility of tracing Miss Ligram's assassin lay solely on his own shoulders, which—as he comfortably assured himself—were quite capable of bearing the burden. He was the more pleased with his employment, as the Grangebury murder case promised to be one of those mysteries which he loved. A dead woman: a strangely furnished room: a pack of cards: these were the elements of the case, and, so far as Gebb could see at present, there was no clue— save the lavish use of the colour yellow—to the past of the victim, or the identity of the assassin. In Mrs. Presk lay his sole hope of gaining intelligence likely to lead to some practical result; so at eleven o'clock next morning Gebb, in an anxious frame of mind, was once more on the scene of the murder, and in the presence of his principal witness.

In the searching light of day Mrs. Presk was more uncomely

than ever. Tall, gaunt, angular, and dressed in the worst possible taste, she presented few of the alluring graces of her sex. To have woo'd, and won, and lived with this strident Amazon, the late Mr. Presk must have been a suitor of no ordinary courage. However, she made an excellent witness, as her brain was clear, her courage high, and she had not a morsel of imagination. Moreover, her hysteria of the previous night had disappeared.

She answered Gebb's leading questions in a cut-and-dried fashion, without discursive rambling after her own private opinions: but with all this, the examination, and the details obtainable therefrom, proved to be anything but satisfactory. Considering the business-like instincts of detective and widow, a more meagre result can scarcely be conceived.

"For how long has Miss Ligram been lodging with you?" was Gebb's first question, put in a form which appeared to assume that the victim was still in existence.

"For three months," replied Mrs. Presk, referring to a dingy little book with which she had furnished herself, in anticipation of the ordeal. "She came to me on the first of May last; she left here—for heaven, I hope—on the twenty-fourth day of July; so, as you can see for yourself, Mr. Gebb, she has been with me two months and twenty-four days, neither more nor less; and there ain't no Court of Law as I'd swear different in."

"She came in answer to an advertisement, I suppose?"

"No, she didn't," contradicted the widow. "I don't advertise: it's low. I put a card in the window, and it was that card which made Miss Ligram apply here for board and lodging. She applied," continued Mrs. Presk, consulting her book, "on the twenty-ninth of April, and I agreed to take her on the thirtieth; so that she entered my house on the first of May."

"Why two days' delay?"

"Because I couldn't make up my mind about taking her in."

"She offered you too little?"

"On the contrary, Mr. Gebb, she offered me too much."

"No wonder you thought her eccentric," said the detective, with irony; "but kindly explain the position more fully."

"I asked her three pound a week for parlour, bedroom, fire, and light, which is little enough, I'm sure, as everything in my house is of the best To my surprise. Miss Ligram offered to pay me six—just double—on condition that I allowed her to dismantle the front room, and refurnish it herself."

"Did she give any reason for this singular request?"

"She said she liked her own goods and chattels about her," replied Mrs. Presk; "and though at first I did not fancy the idea of

16

clearing out the parlour—which was most handsomely furnished—yet, on thinking over the matter, I decided that double the money I asked was not to be despised. I therefore agreed to Miss Ligram's terms, and on the last day of April I dismantled the parlour. On the first of May Miss Ligram came in a van and——"

"Came in a van?" interrupted Gebb, profoundly astonished.

"Yes! she rode beside the driver, and he assisted her to set out the parlour in the style you saw. It was all done in a day by the pair, for Miss Ligram would not let me help."

"Perhaps she was afraid of your asking the driver questions as to where she came from?" suggested Gebb, shrewdly.

"She might have saved herself the trouble," said Mrs. Presk, grimly. "I did speak to the driver, and asked that very question, only to find that he was deaf and dumb."

"Queer!" murmured the detective, rubbing his nose. "She took good care to hide her past I wonder why?"

"I don't," snapped the landlady with feminine malevolence; "it's my opinion that Miss Ligram's past was not respectable."

"H'm! I must say it looks like it. What was the name on the van?"

"There was no name, Mr. Gebb. The van—painted yellow, with one grey horse and a red-headed driver, deaf and dumb—was the private property of Miss Ligram. It was not the first time she had moved that yellow room about," and the widow nodded significantly.

"Why are you doubtful of Miss Ligram's past?"

"Well!" said Mrs. Presk, taking time to answer this question, "you can only judge a person's past by a person's present, and Miss Ligram knew too many shady people for my taste."

"Shady people!" echoed Gebb, pricking up his ears at this hint of a clue; "what sort of people?"

"Fortune-tellers, conjurors, spiritualists, and such-like, sir."

"Ah!" Gebb recalled the spread-out pack of cards, "so she was rather superstitious."

"Superstitious!" cried Mrs. Presk, casting up her eyes. "She was a very pagan for omens, and talismans, and consultation of cards. There wasn't a fortune-teller in London she hadn't down here at one time or another to read her hand, or question the stars, or look into the crystal ball, or spread out the cards. She was a perfect gold mine to those swindlers, believing all their lies, like the poor benighted heathen she was."

"What did she particularly seek to know?"

"The future!" was the landlady's curt reply.

17

"No doubt," returned Gebb, dryly; "and her own future at that. But was there any particular aim in her questioning?"

"Yes!" said Mrs. Presk, with a burst of confidence, "there was. I found it out from one of her fortune-telling visitors. She wanted to know if she would die by violence."

"So!" said Gebb, drawling out the word reflectively in the German fashion. "And was a violent death predicted?"

"It was—by the fortune-teller I asked, Mr. Gebb; and sure enough the prediction came true, though, as a rule, I don't believe in such rubbish; still it was queer she should die with the ace of spades in her lap."

"A fortune-teller was with her on the night she was killed," said Gebb, after a pause.

"How do you know, sir?" questioned Mrs. Presk, eagerly.

"Because the cards were laid out, and the death-card was in the lap of the corpse. Now I believe that this man—— By the way," said Gebb, breaking away from his original speech, "did Miss Ligram smoke?"

"Not to my knowledge," rejoined Mrs. Presk, promptly. "She was a lady in her habits. Some of 'em was queer, but they were all genteel; indeed they were."

"It's not out of keeping with well-bred habits for a lady to smoke," corrected the detective, mildly. "Many ladies do nowadays. But as—according to you—Miss Ligram did not smoke herself, it is probable that her visitor was a man. I found the stump of a cigarette near the chair. When he got behind it to strangle her——"

"To strangle her!" repeated Mrs. Presk, horrified "Do you think this fortune-teller killed her?"

"Yes, I do. I believe firmly that, attracted by her diamonds, he verified his own prediction, and murdered her in the most cold-blooded fashion."

"Impossible, Mr. Gebb. He was a friend of hers!"

"Ah! you know the man!" cried Gebb, pouncing down on this admission.

"No, I don't!" cried the landlady, in rather a nervous manner for one of her iron composure, "but I know she had a visitor on that night. She told me she had a friend coming, but she didn't say if it was a lady or a gentleman. It was because Miss Ligram expected this person that she sent 'Tilda and me to the lecture."

"Sent you to the lecture!" said Gebb, emphasizing the first word.

"Well, she didn't exactly send us," explained Mrs. Presk, reluctantly, "but she gave me two tickets and suggested that we
18

should go. Knowing her habits, and always willing to oblige, I went, and took 'Tilda."

"What do you mean?" asked Gebb, staring at the landlady.

Mrs. Presk explained herself more clearly.

"On occasions Miss Ligram was ashamed of her superstitions, I think, sir, for three or four times she got me and 'Tilda out of the house while she consulted her swindlers. Once," said Mrs. Presk, consulting her book, "it was the Crystal Palace; again, two seats at the Adelphi; Earl's Court Exhibition three weeks ago, and the local lecture last night. But we came back always to find her in bed, until this last time," concluded Mr. Presk, with a shudder.

"A strange woman," commented Gebb, thoughtfully. "So you never found out where she came from?"

"No, sir, she was as close as wax. I called her the Lady from Nowhere."

"You know nothing of her past?"

"Nothing! She might have come from the moon for all I know of her."

"You saw no letters, photographs——"

"Nothing!" interrupted the landlady, emphatically. "I saw nothing."

"Then," said Gebb, rising briskly, "I must stick to the clue of the Yellow Room."

CHAPTER IV

THE FIVE LANDLADIES

The journalist is the true Asmodeus of the day, and is quite as fond as that meddlesome demon of interfering with what does not concern him. He invades the privacy of our lives, unroofs our houses, reveals our secrets, and trumpets forth things best left untold to the four quarters of the globe.

Gebb had an especial abhorrence of this magpie habit of the Press; as he averred, with much reason, that the excessively minute details of criminal cases set forth in the newspapers put the ill-doers on their guard, and warned them of coming dangers, with the result that they were easily able to evade the futile clutches of the hands of Justice. Yet in the instance of the Grangebury murder, the publication of details had a singular result: no less than the assisting of right against wrong.

As soon as the circumstances of the crime became known, the reporters of every newspaper in the metropolis flocked to Paradise Row with expansive notebooks, eager eyes, and inquiring minds. They surveyed the house, questioned the police, interviewed Mrs. Presk, and gave outline portraits of the landlady and her servant. The Yellow Boudoir especially attracted their attention, and stirred their imagination to descriptions of Eastern splendour. It was hinted that its magnificence was on more than a kingly scale; it was compared to the celebrated room in one of Balzac's romances, and its furnishing and appointments were minutely detailed in glowing descriptions, exhausting the most superlative adjectives in the English tongue. Also the unknown history and strange death of its occupant were commented upon; guesses were made as to her identity; and reasons were given for her secretive life, for her strange belief in, and consultation of, charlatans and fortune-tellers and all those cunning gipsies who live by the gullibility of the public. Appeals were made in these articles to the deaf and dumb driver to appear and declare the mystery of the yellow van, the yellow room, and their queer owner. In short, as the journals were in want of a sensation, they made the most of this material supplied by chance, and England from one end to the other rang with the tidings of Miss Ligram's death, Miss Ligram's boudoir, and Miss Ligram's mysterious life. And all this trumpeting and noise, Gebb, the enemy of the Press, heard with singular complacency, indeed, with pleasure and satisfaction.

"As a rule, I hate these revelations," said he to one who knew his views and wondered at his equanimity, "as in nine cases out of ten they do more harm than good by placing the criminal on his guard; but this is the tenth case, where it is advisable to make the details of the crime as public as possible. I rely on these descriptions of the Yellow Boudoir to trace Miss Ligram's past life."

"In what way?" demanded the inquirer.

"In the way of the yellow van," replied Gebb, promptly. "As Mrs. Presk truly observed, the hard fact of that van shows that Miss Ligram was in the habit of moving from place to place with her tent, and setting it up after the fashion of an Arab, in whatever spot took her fancy. Now, when those other people who have had the Yellow Boudoir set out in its tawdry splendour under their roofs read of Miss Ligram's death, and recognize the description of her strange room, they will come forward, and detail their experiences of the lady. So, in one way and another, we may be enabled to trace Miss Ligram's past life back to a starting-point It is the only chance I can see of gaining any knowledge."

Within the week events of a strange nature justified the judicious belief entertained by the astute detective. Letters in female caligraphy were received at Scotland Yard, stating that the writers could give certain information to the police concerning the murdered woman. Also, a few days later, decayed females of the landlady genus presented themselves in person to detail their experiences of Miss Ligram and her eccentricities. From all these personal and written statements it appeared that for four years, more or less, Miss Ligram had been moving from one part of London to another. In no one place she had remained longer than six months, and in each her conduct and mode of life had been the same. She arrived regularly in the yellow van, and, having obtained permission from the various landladies at the cost of paying double the rent demanded, as regularly set up and furnished her Yellow Boudoir. As in the latest instance of the Grangebury episode, she consulted fortune-tellers, spiritualists, and shady people of a like nature, departing at the end of each tenancy without a word as to her destination. It would seem from this evidence that the woman was consistent in her eccentricities, and conducted her strangely secretive life on the most methodical principles.

One thing which seemed of a piece with the dead woman's desire for concealment, was that in every place she—so to speak—camped in, she gave a different name; each appellation being stranger than the last, and all apparently of her own manufacture.

She figured at Hampstead under the name of Margil; in Richmond she was known as Miss Ramlig; when housed in St. John's Wood she called herself Milgar; and at Shepherd's Bush—but for the sake of clearness it will be advisable to let the several landladies speak for themselves—five persons, five pieces of information more or less similar, and five obviously made-up names. So much for the past of Miss Ligram.

Mrs. Brown, of West Kensington, stated that she knew the deceased under the name of Miss Limrag. She arrived at Mrs. Brown's in the month of May, '95, and after a six months' tenancy departed in the month of October in the same year. Mrs. Brown was ignorant as to where she come from, and equally at a loss to declare whither she went. Both in coming and going Miss Limrag used as a means of transport the yellow van, and during her residence she inhabited the Yellow Room of her own furnishing for the consulting therein of the fortune-telling fraternity.

Mrs. Kane testified that a lady who called herself Miss Milgar arrived in Shelley Road, St. John's Wood, on the first day of November, '95, and left the district in the last days of April, '96. Her conduct during her six months' stay was similar to that described by Mrs. Presk and Mrs. Brown. On the evidence of such conduct, and the facts of the van and boudoir (both yellow in colour), Mrs. Kane had no hesitation in declaring that the murdered Miss Ligram, of Grangebury, was her eccentric lodger, Miss Milgar.

The information given by Miss Bain, of Crescent Villa, Hampstead, showed that the name assumed there by the wandering lady was Margil, and that she took possession of her lodgings there in the month of November, '93—having arrived, according to her custom, in the yellow van. While the lodger of Miss Bain, she gave herself up to the study of dream-books, and the interpretation of visions. During her occupancy of Crescent Villa, the landlady, in spite of all efforts, could find out nothing about her past or discover where she came from; and the so-called Miss Margil departed with her furniture towards the end of April, 1894. She left no address.

Miss Lamb, resident at Richmond, entertained the unknown from November, 1894, to April, 1895. She knew her by the strange name of Ramlig, and always thought her weak in her mind, owing to her queer mode of life, and belief in omens. When Miss Ramlig made any boastful speech reflecting on her worldly prosperity, she would touch wood to avert the omen. "Absit omen"; "Umberufen"; "In a good hour be it spoken "; "N'importe." These words and phrases were continually on her tongue; and she was a slave to all forms of superstition. She would not walk under a ladder; if she spilt salt she threw a pinch over her shoulder; an unexpected meeting with a magpie, a hunchback, a cross-eyed person, or with a piebald horse, either made her rejoice in the most extravagant fashion, or threw her into a fever of apprehension. She was not communicative, and resisted all Miss Lamb's attempts at social intercourse. During the whole period of her stay, no words were spoken, and no event occurred, likely to throw light on her past; nor, when she departed, did Miss Lamb discover whither she intended to go. In coming, in staying, in going, Miss Ramlig was a mystery.

The owner of Myrtle Bank, Shepherd's Bush, a bird-like spinster called Cass, informed Gebb that a certain Miss Migral lodged with her from the first of May to the end of October, 1894. She arrived in the van spoken of by the other witnesses; she paid double rent for the privilege of dismantling a room, and therein set up her tent-like habitation of yellow satin, furnished with cane chairs and tables, illuminated with candles, and perfumed with incense. She was, said Miss Cass, superstitious beyond all belief, actually divining by teacups, and believing in the future as foretold by the position of the tea-leaves, after the fashion of illiterate servant-girls. Miss Migral never went to church, she had—so far as Miss Cass knew, no Bible in her possession; but read books dealing with fortune-telling and necromancy. One of her favourite volumes was "The Book of Fate," another "The Book of Dreams," and she appeared to have an insatiable desire to know the future; but for what reason, Miss Cass—in spite of all efforts—was unable to discover. This strange creature departed with all her worldly goods for some unknown destination during the last days of October, 1894.

Mrs. Presk was the last landlady who received this mysterious woman, and knew her as Miss Ligram. She arrived at Paradise Row at the beginning of May, 1896, and met with a violent death three months later. Mrs. Presk was as ignorant of the woman's past as the other landladies had been. She arrived from nowhere, and, no doubt, would have departed six months later in an equally mysterious fashion. But in the middle of her Grangebury tenancy, a violent death put an end to her further wanderings.

Gebb heard all this evidence, which was monotonous from its sameness, with much satisfaction and great attention. By means of the details afforded by the five landladies and Mrs. Presk, he traced back the wanderings of the dead woman to the month of November, 1893, but further back he was unable to go, for lack of information. In spite of all publicity given to the case, notwithstanding advertisements, and his own private efforts, no other witnesses came forward to give evidence as to the past of Miss Ligram; so, finding he was at a dead stop, the detective resolved to stand—at all events for the present—on the information he had already acquired. For his own private information and guidance he tabulated an account of Miss Ligram's names, addresses, and former landladies, together with the dates of her various rests, as follows:—

Miss Bain, Hampstead
Margil, Nov., 1893, to April, 1894

Miss Cass, Shepherd's Bush
Migral, May to Oct.,1894

Miss Lamb, Richmond
Ramlig, Nov., 1894, to April, 1895

Mrs. Brown, West Kensington
Limrag, May to Oct. 1895

Mrs. Kane, St. John's Wool
Milgar, Nov., 1895, to April, 1896

Mrs. Presk, Grangebury
Ligram, April to July, 1896

And at the foot of this table he noted the fact that on the night of the 24th July, 1896—according to medical evidence at ten o'clock—the so-called Miss Ligram met with a violent death at the hands of some unknown person.

So far so good; but here Gebb's information came to an end, and beyond a few years' knowledge of Miss Ligram's past, he had no evidence to show him why she had taken to this mode of life, or why her eccentric manner of living should have been cut short by violence. Ready as he was in resource, the detective did not know how to act, or in which direction to turn for information. While thus perplexed he received a hasty note scribbled on a half-sheet of dirty paper. It ran as follows:—

"48, Guy Street, Pimlico.

"Come and see me at once, about the Grangebury case. I have solved the mystery, and can hang the criminal.—Yours,

Simon Parge."

24

CHAPTER V

A FRIEND IN NEED

But that Gebb knew the writer of this curt note, which was hardly civil in its brevity, he would have been much surprised at the untoward chance of its coming at so critical a moment to help him out of his difficulties. As it was, he felt more relieved than astonished, and hastened to obey the summons without delay. It was not the first time he had used Mr. Parge as a finger-post to point out the right path, and in the present instance he was rather vexed with himself that he had not applied before in this quarter for advice and guidance. But better late than never, thought he, while repairing his error, and making up for his neglect by replying in person to the summons.

Towards Parge, the detective stood in the relation of pupil to master; for it was Parge who, observing his abilities, had induced him to join the profession, and had never ceased to praise, and blame, and help him on to the best of his ability. For some considerable time Parge had been a noted detective himself, and he had retired within the last few years into private life, owing to a tendency to obesity and an increase of years which forbade his further exercising his talents in the way of thief-catching and assassin-hunting. The criminal fraternity had rejoiced rather too soon, when they heard that their great enemy had retired on a pension; for Parge left behind him a worthy successor in the person of Gebb, and he still instructed the latter in particularly difficult cases where two heads were better than one. Mr. Parge, by reason of his eighteen stone, was chained to an armchair for the rest of his life; but his brain was still active, and he took a sufficient interest in Scotland Yard affairs to read all criminal cases, and help his more active deputy to bring them to satisfactory conclusions. The old detective sat in his house like Odin on the Air-throne, and—through the medium of the Press—knew much that was going on in the shady section of society, which he had watched for so many years. Frequently he instructed Gebb how to act, and what conclusions to form on slender evidence; and the pupil, when at a loss, invariably turned to his master for a word of encouragement and explanation. But that Parge had forestalled him by sending the note, Gebb, later on, would have laid the case of the Yellow Boudoir before his—so to speak—sleeping partner.

"I guess the old man will be in a rage," said Gebb to himself as he hurried with all speed to Pimlico. "I should have seen him before on the matter, only it has bothered me so. He says he has solved the mystery—that means he has discovered who killed Miss Ligram. I don't believe it—with the greatest possible respect for Simon—I don't believe it."

The ex-detective dwelt in a little house in a little square, and passed his time usually in a huge armchair, placed conveniently near the window, so that he could survey the busy world from which he had withdrawn. He was a Daniel Lambert for size and rotundity, with a large red face like a full moon, and an impressive girth which would have made the fortune of an alderman; but his eyes were keen and bright, and the brain pertaining to this man-mountain of flesh was as active as one cased in the leanest of bodies. He was clothed in a gaudy-figured dressing-gown of blue and red, wore carpet slippers on his large feet, a smoking-cap with a large tassel on his sparse locks, and sat amid a litter of newspapers. Parge took in nearly every morning and evening journal in London, and from dawn till dark read the police news, cutting out all such cases as he deemed worthy of his attention. In the evening he usually played whist with his wife and two cronies, or kept the company enthralled by his stories of the scoundrels he had exposed, and the under-world he had moved in. Mrs. Parge—an anæmic woman, as slender as Simon was stout—waited on her husband, and thought him—intellectually and morally, as he was physically—the greatest of men. She did all the house-work with the assistance of a small servant, and, being an excellent cook, had contributed not a little to the weight and size of her spouse by preparing those appetizing dishes which her Simon loved. The couple had a comfortable income, a comfortable house, and both enjoyed the best of health, so that the Parge household was as happy a one as could be found in London.

"My word, Absalom," said lean Mrs. Parge when she opened the door, "you're going to have a bad time; you've going to catch it. Simon saw you from the window, and is getting up steam to receive you."

A series of growls proceeding from the near parlour proclaimed the truth of this warning, and when Gebb entered the presence of his master, steam was got up so far that Parge's smoking-cap came skimming past the head of the visitor. Gebb picked it up and brought it to Parge, who received him and it with a growl of wrath. At Parge's feet lay a pile of newspapers, some open, some folded, some with evidence of scissors' work and some quite whole. On a near table there lay a large volume bound in red cloth, which Gebb recognized as one of the series of books in which Parge noted down the more important cases, and stored his newspaper cuttings. He wondered if the old man had it at his elbow to throw at him, for Parge's fingers evidently itched to send the book after the smoking-cap; but, as he refrained from further violence, Gebb concluded that the volume had been placed within reach of its owner for some purpose connected with his visit. He was right, as subsequent events proved.

"Oh!" growled Parge, glaring at the young man, "so you've thought fit to come at last?"

"I couldn't come sooner, Simon," protested Gebb, taking a chair, "I've been worried out of my life by this Grangebury case."

"And what good has all your worry done, you fool? You've found out nothing."

"Indeed I have. I've traced back Miss Ligram's life to the year '93. She is—but I forget—you don't know the case."

"Don't I!" retorted Parge, sharply. "I know a deal more than you can tell me. I suppose you are in difficulties over the matter?"

Gebb admitted that he was. "And I candidly confess that I do not see my way out of them," he added, with an anxious look at Parge.

The fat man grunted. "If you had come to me in the first instance I could have saved you a lot of trouble."

"Can you explain the mystery, Simon?"

"I can. If I couldn't, I wouldn't have sent for you."

"Do you know the motive for the committal of the crime?"

"I do I've employed my wits to some purpose, I can tell you."

"And the name of the assassin?"

"Yes! Didn't I say in my letter that I had solved the mystery, you fool?"

"And where he is to be found?" continued Gebb, exhaustively.

For the first time Parge replied in the negative. "There you have me," he grumbled, scratching his chin. "I know where he should be, but I don't know where he is. It will be your business to find him."

"If you'll give me a clue to his whereabouts, I'll do my best," was the meek reply of the pupil.

"I can't," said the ex-detective, frankly. "I did my best to hunt him down four years ago, before I retired, and I failed."

"Ho! Ho! So this cove has been in trouble before?"

"Not only in trouble, but in prison."

"On what charge?" asked Gebb, with openly expressed surprise.

"On a charge of murder!"

"What! Is this assassination of Miss Ligram his second crime?"

"It is," replied Parge, enjoying the astonishment of his visitor;

27

"but this man—I'll tell you his name later on—did not intend to kill Miss Ligram."

"But he did kill her—strangled her!"

"Not Miss Ligram!" said the fat man, obstinately. "Ligram was an assumed name."

"I know that, Simon. She has passed under half a dozen names."

"So the papers say. Just run over the names."

Gebb did so promptly, giving the names in order. "Margil, Migral, Ramlig, Limrag, Milgar, and Ligram."

"Good! Now, Absalom, what strikes you as strange about these names?"

"They are all invented," said Gebb, after a pause.

"Quite so," assented Parge, "and their invention does credit to the imagination of the lady. Do you notice that the same letters, differently placed, are used in every instance?"

"Anagrammatic!" said Gebb, with a nod.

"Precisely! She manufactured all these false names out of her real one."

"A very ingenious idea, Simon. And what is her real name?"

"Gilmar!" replied Parge, slowly. "Miss Ellen Gilmar, of Kirkstone Hall, near Norminster, Hants."

For quite two minutes Gebb sat in silence, looking at his chief in blended wonder and amazement Try as he might he could not guess how the fat man had come by this knowledge. What he, with the use of his limbs, and the power of the law, had failed to discover, this invalid—as he might be called—had found out without moving from his armchair. In a darker age Gebb might have judged Parge to be gifted with necromantic power, or divination by second sight.

"Are you certain of this?" he asked in a hesitating voice.

"Quite certain!" cried Parge, furiously. "Quite certain. I'm not a fool."

"But how did you find out?"

"By exercising my memory and joining the past with the present."

"In what way?" asked Gebb, still perplexed "What clue had you?"

"The clue of the Yellow Boudoir."

"The Yellow Boudoir!" repeated Gebb, recalling his own fancy.

"Yes!" said Parge, gravely "Twenty years ago, in a room furnished in the same fashion, in a room under the roof of Kirkstone Hall, there was a murder committed. In this book," Parge here laid his hand on the large volume, "there is a full account of the trial of

28

one, Marmaduke Dean, for the murder of John Kirkstone; and the crime was committed in the Yellow Boudoir."

"But what has a crime committed twenty years ago to do with the assassination of Miss Lig—I mean, of Miss Gilmar?"

"Everything. Miss Gilmar only reaped as she sowed. You must hear the story in full before you can see the connection. But to put the matter briefly, you must understand that Dean was convicted of killing Kirkstone and was sentenced to death. Afterwards, as there was some doubt about the absolute justice of the verdict, the death sentence was commuted to penal servitude for life. Dean swore that he was innocent, and that the accomplishment of the crime had been brought about by the machinations of Ellen Gilmar. He swore, if his life were spared, to escape from prison and kill the woman who had placed him by her craft and cruelty in the dock. About four years ago the man did escape from Dartmoor Prison; and it was dread lest he should keep his word which drove Miss Gilmar from lodging to lodging, under different names. For some reason—best known to herself—she chose to dwell in a room, furnished and draped similar to that in which the first crime had been committed. It was reading the description of that room which put me on the right track.

"And you believe that Miss Ligram and Miss Gilmar are one and the same person?" asked Gebb, breathlessly.

"I am certain of it, on the authority of the Yellow Boudoir."

"And you think that Dean murdered her?"

"Yes; I believe that Dean kept his word."

"But what was his reason?"

"Vengeance!" said Parge, opening the red book. "Listen! I will tell you the case after my own fashion, and you shall learn the reason why Miss Ligram was strangled at Grangebury."

CHAPTER VI

THE CRIME OF KIRKSTONE HALL

It sometimes happens that a youthful spendthrift becomes an aged miser, and hoards money in the same extreme fashion as formerly he wasted it. John Kirkstone was a fair example of this species of human chameleon. As his father's heir, he drained the estate of all ready money, and squandered the same in London without regard to economy or even reason. In this riotous life he was encouraged by a former college companion—one Marmaduke Dean—who even went to the extent of borrowing money of Kirkstone, and so became his debtor for a large sum. Dean subsequently married a lady of fortune, and repaid a portion of the money; but either could not, or—as was more probable—would not discharge the whole. On this point Kirkstone, who needed money for his pleasures, quarrelled with his friend, and the pair parted to meet no more for some years. It would have been better for both had they never renewed their youthful friendship.

As might be expected, old Squire Kirkstone was by no means pleased with his son, and did not relish leaving his large fortune to one who probably would waste it in a few years. The Hall and its surrounding acres were entailed, and were bound to pass into John Kirkstone's hands; but the old man possessed a large income acquired by speculation, which was at his own disposal. Wrathful at his spendthrift son, he resolved to leave this personal property to his only daughter; and accordingly, when John became Squire on the death of his father, he found that his sister Laura was in possession of a good income, while he had to be content with a dwelling far too large for his means, and several farms whose tenants did not always pay their rents. The shock of this discovery was unpleasant, but salutary.

In the first place Kirkstone renounced his London profligacy and associates, and came to live at the Hall; in the second, he insisted that his sister should dwell with him, and pay a handsome yearly sum for the privilege; and in the third, he invited his first cousin, Ellen Gilmar, to be his housekeeper. Laura Kirkstone, who was a weak-bodied and weak-natured girl, readily consented to remain at the Hall, and pay what her brother demanded, and as readily welcomed her cousin Ellen as mistress of the household, a post for which she herself had no great love. Having thus arranged matters, Kirkstone—though not yet forty—became as penurious as formerly he had been wasteful; and in this system of economy was ably assisted by his new housekeeper, a shrewd, cold-hearted skinflint.

Laura, in derision, called Ellen Mrs. Harpagon, after Molière's miser; and well did Miss Gilmar deserve the name. She was a little, black, active woman, with a neat figure and a somewhat pinched white face. Her eyes were hard-looking, her lips were thin, and she was a perfect skinflint in the management of the household. Even Kirkstone, inclined as he was to economy, grumbled at times about her excessive economy; but as the months went by, he fell gradually into her saving way of living, and the Hall soon gained a name in the county for all that was mean and niggardly. The larder was always kept locked, the servants were ill fed, and the occasional beggars who came to that forbidden door were not fed at all. Scraping, and screwing, and hoarding of money became the order of the day; and Kirkstone soon found that he was redeeming his former waste, at the cost of a hard and somewhat hungry life. However, the habit of living thus penuriously became confirmed, and both he and Mrs. Harpagon vied with one another in discovering new methods of saving money. The only person in the Hall who did not relish this extreme economy was Laura Kirkstone.

The attitude adopted by Kirkstone towards his wealthy sister was a fairly amiable one. Having a strong will, he compelled her weaker one to bow to it; and kept a sharp watch on her, lest she should marry some one of whom he did not approve, and so take the money—which he looked upon as rightfully his own—out of the family. Many a young man would have been glad to marry Miss Kirkstone, both for her money and good looks; for in a pink-and-white sort of way the girl was pretty; but Kirkstone invited none of these would-be suitors to the house, and turned a cold shoulder to them in public. Laura was forbidden even to speak to them; and being kept closely to her own home, lived in the gaunt, grim Hall, like an enchanted princess guarded by two ogres. And none of the young knights who wished to marry her had sufficient courage to brave the black looks of Kirkstone, or the acidulated sneers of his amiable housekeeper and cousin. Such was the position of affairs at Kirkstone Hall when Marmaduke Dean again entered into the life of his former friend.

It was the death of his wife which led to Dean's visit to Kirkstone Hall. He had squandered the fortune of the unhappy lady, and had treated her with so much coldness and neglect that she had died of a broken heart, leaving him a little son. Dean promptly placed the child with some distant relatives, and being poor again,

31

looked about him for some means whereby he could procure money. Recalling the easy-going and generous disposition of Kirkstone, he resolved to apply to him for aid, quite oblivious to the fact that he was already in his debt. To this end he one day presented himself at the Hall, and was astonished to find that its owner, from a generous friend, had changed into a miserly curmudgeon. Kirkstone not only refused to help Dean, but demanded immediate repayment of the monies already due. Dean, seeing that only trouble would come of his application, was on the point of withdrawing, so as to save himself the danger of being sued for the lent money, when a new idea entered into Kirkstone's knavish brain which made him detain Dean at the Hall as a necessary element to bring it to fruition. The scheme was none other than the marriage of Laura to the disconsolate widower, and comprehended a division of her fortune between the brother and the proposed husband, an amiable arrangement which really amounted to robbery.

Laura herself forced Kirkstone to adopt this plan by reason of her refusal to let him handle the fortune which had been left to her by their father. Like most weak-minded people she was singularly obstinate on some points, and, being cunning enough to see that her sole hold over her brother lay in retaining command of her money, she always evaded his proposals to manage her investments. Beyond the income he derived from the sum she paid for board and lodging, Kirkstone had nothing to do with these monies, of which, as he frequently stated, he had been robbed. Naturally he was angered to think of his loss, and tried several times to bully Laura into surrendering her fortune. The result of this ill-judged conduct was that Laura met force by cunning, and, taking a dislike to her brother, executed a secret will, whereby she left the whole of the money to Ellen Gilmar.

In this case there was no honour among thieves, for the housekeeper tricked her master and cousin by keeping secret the fact of the will, and when Kirkstone tried to marry his sister to Dean, he was quite unaware that Ellen, for her own selfish ends, intended to thwart the match if she could. Furthermore a new and unforeseen obstacle arose to complicate matters, for it chanced that both Laura and Ellen fell in love with Dean. The scamp was a handsome man, with a plausible manner, and Laura was quite willing to marry him, and to settle half her fortune on him, receiving in return a presentable husband with a damaged reputation. It was agreed between Kirkstone and Dean that when the marriage took place the latter should discharge his debt to the former, and also pay over a certain sum of money by way of commission on the marriage settlement. So far all went well, and Kirkstone invited Dean to stay at the Hall until the marriage took place, and all pecuniary arrangements between them were settled. It was then that Ellen threw prudence to the wind, and lost her heart to Dean.

The result of this feminine weakness was that Ellen did violence to her instincts by relaxing her stingy rule. She kept the table supplied with better food while Dean stayed at the Hall, she paid more attention to her dress, humoured the man she loved in every way, and altogether behaved in a manner so alien to her natural self that Laura became suspicious. The end of this folly was that Laura discovered Ellen's secret, and lost her temper over it. She accused Dean of making love to Ellen, and Ellen of encouraging his advances. Kirkstone was told this by his sister, and he, seeing a chance of his losing money by the marriage not taking place, had a stormy scene with Ellen. He threatened to turn her out of the Hall as a pauper; whereat the woman turned at bay on her cousin, and revealed the truth about the secret will.

"If this marriage takes place," she declared, "I lose money as well as you, and if I can influence Laura to refuse Dean I shall certainly do so. If it comes to the point, we shall see who is the stronger, you or I."

The upshot of this conversation was that Kirkstone lost his temper altogether, and went to bully his sister into revoking her will. Had he only remembered that the same result would be attained by the marriage taking place, he would have urged on the match and defied Ellen. Instead of acting thus sensibly, he vented his rage on Dean, and accused him of encouraging the folly of the housekeeper. Then Dean lost his temper in his turn, and quarrelled with Kirkstone and Laura; so in the month of July, '76, it chanced that the four people inhabiting Kirkstone Hall quite misunderstood one another, and, for the time being, were hardly on speaking terms. Dean stormed at Kirkstone as trying to thwart the proposed marriage; Kirkstone blamed Dean as having encouraged the love of Ellen; and Laura, in her weak way, fretted herself ill over the whole disturbance. Only Ellen, the cause of all the trouble, retained her placidity. She did not move an inch from her position. She had an end to gain, and in one way or another she was determined to gain it. It was while things were in this unhappy state that the country was startled by the news that Kirkstone had been murdered by Dean.

The tragedy took place in a certain room strangely furnished by the mother of the present squire, which was known as the Yellow Boudoir. It was a favourite apartment with Kirkstone, who had turned it into a smoking-room. On the night of the 16th of July, Kirkstone and Dean were drinking and smoking in this room, when apparently they renewed their quarrel with a fatal result Kirkstone was found dead in the room at midnight with a knife in his heart. This knife had been brought from America—it was a bowie-knife—by Dean, and his name was marked on the handle. Ellen deposed at the inquest that, guessing the pair might quarrel, she had gone downstairs shortly before midnight to implore them to part. Then she had seen Dean leave the Yellow Boudoir in a state of alarm and alcoholic excitement. Afterwards Kirkstone asked her to tell Dean to come down again. She did so, and Dean rejoined Kirkstone. When they parted for the second time Ellen went to the smoking-room, and found Kirkstone lying dead with Dean's knife in his heart The result of this statement was that Dean was arrested for the murder of his friend, and, mainly on the evidence of Miss Gilmar, he was found guilty. The man protested his innocence in vain, and would have suffered the extreme penalty of the law, but that a sympathizing section of the public, not satisfied with the judgment, prepared a memorial to the Home Secretary. The sentence was then commuted to penal servitude for life.

The immediate result of the crime was that Laura, on seeing the dead body of her brother, and learning that the man she loved had murdered him, received such a shock that within three months she was dead. As her will in favour of Ellen had never been revoked, the former housekeeper came in for all her money. Also, as no male heirs of the Kirkstone family were left, Miss Gilmar, by the will of her great-great-grandfather, and as the daughter of John Kirkstone's paternal aunt; inherited the estates. Therefore Ellen Gilmar lost the man she loved, but found herself a wealthy and lonely woman. Only one thing she feared, and that was a violent death; for Dean had declared that his unjust sentence was due to her lying evidence, and that, if his life were spared, he would some day kill her. Apparently he had done so.

Such was the statement of the Kirkstone Hall Crime, which was undoubtedly in some secret way connected with the more recent murder of Ellen Gilmar at Grangebury. The question was—did Dean strangle her out of revenge, since he had escaped from prison about the time Miss Gilmar left the Hall on her lonely wanderings, and was at large to carry out his threat?

If Dean murdered Kirkstone he would have no compunction in committing a second crime to revenge himself on the woman who had delivered him into the hands of Justice.

If Dean did not murder Kirkstone it might be that, enraged at his unjust sentence, he had killed Miss Gilmar to punish her for the lying evidence which had smirched his name and ruined his life.

In either case there was the threat to murder Miss Gilmar,

which, on the face of it, implicated the convict in the Grangebury murder. Deeming the man guilty of the first crime, Parge declared that he had committed the second.

Putting aside the first crime, Gebb maintained that Dean was innocent It now remains to discover which of the two is in the right.

CHAPTER VII

COMMENTS ON THE CRIME

It must not be supposed that in informing Gebb of these details in connection with a long-forgotten crime, Parge gave the exact context of the newspaper reports. He used them rather as notes to refresh his memory, and detailed the somewhat barren information in a conversational manner, adding, suppressing, and amplifying evidence in the way most necessary to convey a clear idea of the case to his hearer. Yet at the conclusion of his reading, or rather narrative, Gebb was not satisfied. To him the case seemed incomplete.

"I know a good deal of what happened before the murder," he said bluntly, "but very little about the crime itself."

"You know all that was reported in the newspapers," replied the fat man, casting the heavy book on the table with some irritation.

"Probably; but now I wish to know such details as were not given to the public You can supply them."

"Certainly! Ask what you like, and I'll answer. You'll arrive at an understanding of the case soonest that way."

Gebb remained silent for a few minutes, and watched Parge lighting his pipe. Then he asked suddenly, "Do you believe that Dean is innocent of this Kirkstone Hall crime?"

"No!" replied Parge, deliberately, "I don't."

"On what grounds?"

"On the grounds of his defence."

"H'm!" said Gebb, with an astonished look; "those are queer grounds on which to doubt a man."

"Well, Absalom, you can judge for yourself. Dean declared that he was innocent."

"They all do; and no doubt, having regard to this new crime, he said that Miss Gilmar was guilty."

"No, he did not accuse her. He ascribed the crime to Laura."

"What! to the sister?"

"Yes! the mean hound, to the woman he was about to marry. Is not such a foul accusation enough to make you believe the wretch to be guilty?"

"Not quite," rejoined Gebb, dryly; "a man may be a blackguard without being a murderer. Besides, this Laura seems to have been weak—in fact, half-witted; so Dean might have had some grounds for his belief. However, if you can recall his defence, I shall be in a better position to judge."

"Briefly," replied Parge, "his defence was as follows. He declared that he was left alone with Kirkstone in the Yellow Boudoir, or rather smoking-room, about half-past ten o'clock."

"Who left him and Kirkstone alone?"

"The ladies. They accompanied the two from the drawing-room, and chatted with them for a few moments before saying good night."

"What!" cried Gebb, suspiciously, "in spite of the disturbed atmosphere of the house, and the quarrelling?"

"Yes! there existed, it seemed, a kind of armed neutrality, and, notwithstanding the situation, the quartet were civil enough to one another."

"I have my doubts about so improbable a situation," said Gebb, shaking his head. "Well, and what took place after the ladies retired?"

"Kirkstone and Dean quarrelled over the marriage. Kirkstone, it seemed, began to taunt Dean about his attentions to Miss Gilmar. Dean turned round, and declared that he was not attached to Miss Gilmar; nor, for the matter of that, to Laura. Both women, he said, were in love with him, and he could marry either without consulting Kirkstone. He furthermore swore that if Kirkstone insulted him any more, he would marry Laura without her brother's consent, and refuse to pay the money."

"And no doubt at this point Kirkstone lost his temper," suggested Gebb.

"So Dean declared; and the quarrel reached such a pitch that Dean——"

"Killed Kirkstone," finished Gebb, quickly.

"No," replied Parge; "he denied that. He left the room, according to his own story, about eleven o'clock, and retired to his bedroom. Shortly before midnight, when he was considering how to act, Ellen Gilmar knocked at his door and said that Kirkstone wanted to see him in the smoking-room. Dean descended and found Kirkstone dead. At first he was tempted to give the alarm; but reflecting on the quarrel, which must have been overheard by some of the servants—a fact afterwards proved—and finding that the knife with which the crime had been committed was his own, he fled back to his room. Then Miss Gilmar came to see what had occurred— found the dead body, and gave the alarm. She accused Dean of being the murderer, because she had left Kirkstone alive when she brought the message, and afterwards found him dead when Dean fled from the room."

37

"But how did Dean implicate Laura?"

"He declared that he had given her the bowie-knife at her own request to prune some plants with in the conservatory."

"Now, that is ridiculous!" cried Gebb.

"Of course it is; and a further proof of his own guilt Ladies don't use bowie-knives to prune plants. Dean, however, stated that he left Kirkstone alive when he first retired to his room. Miss Gilmar stated that her cousin was not dead when she conveyed the message to Dean: so for the defence it was maintained that between the time Miss Gilmar left Kirkstone and the time Dean returned to the Yellow Room for the second visit, Laura must have killed her brother with the bowie-knife, which she had obtained two days previously from Dean."

"But why should Laura kill her brother?"

"Because, as prisoner's counsel argued, it was probable that after the last conversation, Kirkstone fancied that Dean might not pay the money if the marriage came off, so he resolved to stop it by exercising his influence over Laura while there was yet time. Laura, so Dean declared, must have revolted and killed Kirkstone in a moment of uncontrollable anger."

"Still, why should she bring the knife into the smoking-room if she committed the crime on the impulse of the moment?"

"Dean did not—could not—explain that point," replied Parge, with contempt; "all his defence was that he gave Laura the bowie-knife, that he left Kirkstone alive in the Yellow Boudoir about eleven, and that when summoned by Miss Gilmar he found the man dead. Also, that he held his tongue because he was afraid of being accused, as there had been a quarrel between himself and Kirkstone."

"I don't wonder he was afraid," said Gebb, thoughtfully; "and in any case his defence was extremely weak. What evidence did the prosecution bring forward?"

"Miss Gilmar was their principal witness, as she was the last person to see Kirkstone alive. She denied any knowledge of the bowie-knife; but stated that she had come downstairs to prevent further quarrelling. Kirkstone was alone, but asked her to request Dean to come back to the Yellow Boudoir. She went up to Dean's room and asked him. At first he refused, but later on consented. It was twenty minutes between the time Miss Gilmar left Kirkstone alive and Dean found his dead body. One point of the evidence against Dean was that blood was found on his shirt-cuff. He explained this away by stating that he had felt Kirkstone's heart to see if any life remained, and so got his cuffs soiled with the blood from the wound."

38

"What did Laura say to Dean's accusation?"

"She denied it altogether. But it was the horror of thinking that the man she loved deemed her capable of such a foul crime which was one of the causes to bring about her death."

"She was half-witted, you say?" said Gebb, after a pause.

"No!" replied Parge, sharply. "I don't say so. She was weak-witted and soft-natured, but, as I truly believe, perfectly sane. I see that you think she might have killed her brother in a fit of insane rage. Well, that was Dean's defence; or at least part of it. But Laura, when in the witness-box, declared that after leaving Dean and her brother in the Yellow Boudoir she had not left her room all night; and in this statement she was supported by Miss Gilmar. Now you can see for yourself, Gebb, that Dean was rightfully convicted."

"Well," said the detective, reflectively, "it looks like justice; but it may not be so. For my part, knowing what I do of women, I should not be at all surprised to learn that Miss Gilmar was the guilty person."

"Some people suggested as much at the time," said Parge, in no wise disturbed by this suggestion. "But I did not believe it then, and I don't now. What possible motive could she have?"

"Quite as feasible a motive as the one ascribed to Laura," replied Gebb. "Did not Kirkstone threaten to turn her out-of-doors? Was it not his intention to deprive Miss Gilmar of Dean by marrying him to Laura? And did he not try to induce Laura to revoke her will in favour of the housekeeper? Oh, there are plenty of motives."

"But when do you suggest she committed the crime?"

"Why, between the time Dean left the Yellow Room and returned to it again. I dare say she had a row with Kirkstone on her own account, and killed him, then went up to Dean with a lying message to implicate him in the matter."

"But," objected Parge, again, "why should she accuse Dean? He was the man she loved."

"Yes; but he did not love her, and no doubt since she was old and ill-favoured, he showed his dislike to her advances too plainly. I fancy that it was a case of a woman scorned, and that Miss Gilmar revenged herself by accusing Dean. However, this is all theory," added Gebb, with a shrug, "and, as such, is worth little. Dean was condemned on Miss Gilmar's testimony, and, no doubt, intended to kill her if he could escape. Although," added the detective, inconsequently, "I don't believe he did."

"Why not?" said Parge, emphatically. "He did escape, and I believe he did kill her. As sure as I sit here, it was Dean who strangled that wretched woman."

"Humph! Humph!" said Gebb, perplexed. "I'm not certain."

"I am, Absalom. Why, she expected to meet with a violent death at his hands. That was why she left Kirkstone Hall, and concealed herself in these various lodgings under several false names. Besides, as I read in the papers, she constantly consulted fortune-tellers as to whether she would die by violence: a behaviour which showed how lively were her fears."

"That is all very well," admitted Gebb, "but there was no struggle: there was wine drunk; a cigarette smoked by the murderer: and Miss Gilmar let him wander about the room. What does all this prove? That she knew her visitor and trusted him. She could not, and would not, have trusted the man who had sworn to kill her."

"He might have gone to her disguised as a fortune-teller," suggested Parge.

"That is rather an imaginative suggestion," said Gebb, smiling. "By the way, when did Dean escape?"

"Towards the end of '93; and you say yourself that Miss Gilmar began her wanderings in that year."

"Quite so; and I admit that she fled to escape Dean's vengeance, but I am not so certain that he killed her. Remember, the diamonds were stolen; so it may be a vulgar murder for robbery, after all."

"No," said Parge, sticking obstinately to his point. "Dean killed her out of revenge, and stole the diamonds to provide himself with the means of escape. Have you been round the pawnshops?"

"Not yet; but every pawnbroker has been warned. Also, I have sent detectives over to Amsterdam and to Paris to watch if the diamonds turn up."

"Very good," said Simon, with a nod; "if Dean tries to pawn the jewels you'll catch him."

"I don't believe the thief is Dean."

"I do; and also that he killed Miss Gilmar. Well, and what do you intend to do now?"

"Go down to Kirkstone Hall and see the original of the Yellow Boudoir."

"Good! And afterwards?"

"Interview the solicitor who conducted the defence for Dean."

"You mean the barrister."

"No, I don't; I mean the solicitor. Who was Dean's solicitor?"

"Mr. Prain, of 40, Bacon Lane. You won't get anything out of him, Absalom," said Parge, warningly. "He's as close as wax."

"Who was Dean's counsel?" asked Gebb, ignoring the hint.

"Clement Basson," replied Parge; "you'll induce him to talk freely—for a drink."

"Oh! he is dissipated?"

"In a sort of way. A Bohemian barrister: ruined his career through love of pleasure. Has had a few briefs, but not enough to pay, and lives on a small income."

Gebb noted this nutshell biography in his pocket-book, and prepared to take his departure. He had a parting glass with the fat man, and after promising to advise him of all that took place in connection with the case, he left the house.

"And tell me!" cried Parge after him, obstinate to the last; "tell me when you find Dean."

CHAPTER VIII

MR. PRAIN, SOLICITOR

When Gebb left Parge he intended to go down to Norminster with as little delay as possible and look over Kirkstone Hall. There he hoped to learn further details of Miss Gilmar's life, and to ascertain, if possible, whether she had other enemies besides the man she had condemned to lifelong imprisonment. Owing to her grasping disposition and penurious mode of life, it was probable that she had been extremely unpopular, and it might be that amongst those who disliked her might be found one who had carried the feeling so far as to kill her.

On considering the circumstances of the case Gebb could not bring himself to believe that Dean was the assassin. All the same he was anxious to ascertain the hiding-place of the convict, and make certain of his innocence of this second crime; with the first, which was before his time, he had nothing to do.

On second thoughts, however, the detective judged it would be wiser to call on Mr. Prain beforehand, and learn his opinion on the matter. Also, Gebb wished to discover why the solicitor had not come forward to identify the body of Miss Gilmar. From the description of the Yellow Boudoir, so often referred to in the papers, he must have been aware that the so-called Miss Ligram was none other than Ellen Gilmar. If so, why had he not assisted the police to trace the woman's past history? It was mainly to elucidate this point—which might be an important one in solving the mystery— that Gebb called at the office in Bacon Lane.

Mr. Prain proved to be a small, lean-faced man, with a sharp pair of eyes and a hard-looking mouth. He was neatly and spotlessly dressed in the plainest fashion, and his office, a somewhat dingy place, was as clear and trim as himself. When Gebb sent in his card Mr. Prain had only to glance at the name to know that his visitor was the Scotland Yard detective, and told the clerk to show him in at once. It was with his hard little face set like a mask that Prain received the officer of the law, for he had quite expected sooner or later to receive such a visit, and was not unprepared.

"You wish to see me, Mr. Gebb?" said the solicitor, in a low crisp voice.

"Yes, sir; about a case you dealt with twenty years ago."

"Oh! Then you have no questions to ask about the case of to-day?" said Prain, composedly, and he darted a sharp look at his visitor to see how the shot told.

"Do you know my errand?" asked Gebb, somewhat uncomfortably, for he was by no means pleased to find that the little solicitor was prepared for his reception, and could not conceive why it should be so.

"Yes, Mr. Gebb, I do. If you had not called on me, it is probable that I should have paid you a visit."

"It is two weeks since the crime was committed, Mr. Prain; so you have had ample time to call."

"No doubt," returned Prain, dryly, "but it so chanced that I was abroad in Italy. However, when I saw the description of the Yellow Boudoir I hastened back at once."

"You guessed by the description of the yellow room that the murdered woman was Miss Gilmar."

"I did! But may I ask how you found it out?"

"An ex-detective told me. He traced her identity by the same means as you did. But for his recollection of the room I should have known nothing."

"Oh! So the Yellow Boudoir gave Parge the clue," said Prain, thoughtfully.

"Yes! But how did you guess that I referred to Parge?"

"He was the detective employed by the prosecution to hang my client; but he did not succeed, for Dean still lives."

"Ah, does he? Do you know where he is to be found?" asked Gebb, sharply.

"No!" replied Prain, shaking his head. "I know that he escaped about four years ago, and that Miss Gilmar, out of fear of him, left Kirkstone Hall lest he should kill her; I know no more."

"You know one thing at least," retorted Gebb, astonished at the coolness of the man, "that Dean killed Miss Gilmar."

"I deny that," said Prain, sharply; then after a pause, he added, "Do you know why I came back to England on reading about her death?"

"No, I do not! How should I?"

"And why I intended to call on you?"

"No! You'll have to answer your own questions, Mr. Prain."

"Then I'll tell you," said the solicitor, slowly. "I wish to find out if Miss Gilmar left a confession behind her stating why, and how, she killed John Kirkstone; it was for that reason I returned so quickly."

"Miss Gilmar kill Kirkstone?" cried Gebb, thinking of his own suspicions. "Why, even your unhappy client did not accuse her."

"My unhappy client, as you call him, was a fool," retorted Prain, coolly; "he thought that Laura Kirkstone was guilty, whereas I am sure that the housekeeper killed her master. But I could not bring the crime home to her, and Dean was condemned to penal servitude on account of a murder which I am certain he did not commit. When I heard of his escape I thought he might find out Miss Gilmar and make her confess. He always intended to escape, if possible, for that purpose."

Gebb thought for a moment. "Perhaps he killed her, after all, because she would not confess," said he, with some hesitation.

"No," replied Prain. "Dean was wild and wasteful, and, between you and me, Mr. Gebb, not altogether as well-behaved as he might have been, but I am sure he was not the man to commit a murder. Believe me, he is as innocent of this second crime as he was of the first."

"Well," said Gebb, thoughtfully, "I have my doubts regarding his guilt in both cases. I agree with you, going by the story told to me by Parge, that Miss Gilmar killed Kirkstone, but who killed Miss Gilmar?"

"Some unknown person, for the sake of the diamonds," returned Prain, promptly.

"The diamonds?"

"Yes. Miss Gilmar took possession of Laura Kirkstone's jewels, and amongst them were some valuable diamonds. I read in the papers that Miss Gilmar wore those diamonds nightly, and that when her dead body was discovered the diamonds were gone."

"True enough," replied Gebb, "It might be a case of robbery, as you say. But if the murderer tries to dispose of those diamonds by sale or pawning, I'll be able to catch him."

"I may tell you," said Prain, after some reflection, "that the most valuable of Laura's jewels was a diamond necklace, which I see by the reports in the papers was stolen by the murderer. Now, that necklace was given to Laura by Dean, and Miss Gilmar had no right to it."

"But how could Dean, who was almost bankrupt, afford to give Laura a diamond necklace?"

"The necklace was a family jewel," said the solicitor, quickly; "and I have a description of it. This I shall have copied and give it to you; it may assist you to trace the necklace."

"And thereby snare the murderer," answered Gebb. "Thank you, Mr. Prain; the description you speak of will be very serviceable. And now I wish to ask you a few questions about Miss Gilmar, if you don't mind replying to them?"

"Why should I mind?" retorted Prain, raising his eyebrows.

"Parge gave me to understand you were as close as wax," said Gebb, pointedly. "I use his own words."

Prain shrugged his shoulders. "I don't deny it," he said quietly. "Why should I? Twenty years ago I was trying to save Dean from being hanged, while Parge was doing his best to place the rope round the man's neck. Naturally, I was on my guard, and refused to tell Parge all I knew. Your position is a different one, Mr. Gebb; as, with me, you desire to learn the name of Miss Gilmar's murderer. I am quite at your service, and you can ask me what you please."

"Thank you. Then tell me who inherits Miss Gilmar's property?"

"Do you mean her real or personal estate?" asked Prain.

"Both," replied Gebb, promptly.

"Well, then, you must know that the Kirkstone estates were entailed; but the entail ended with that first murder."

"So I heard from Parge, Mr. Prain. In the male line."

"Yes, in the male line. Afterwards, by the will of the Kirkstone who bought them, and who lived some hundred and fifty years ago, they pass on through the female line. Now, the male line died out with John Kirkstone, so that the estates passed by the will to the female line, represented by Laura. When she died Ellen Gilmar inherited through her mother, who was Kirkstone's aunt on the paternal side. Now that Miss Gilmar is dead the estates pass to John Alder, a barrister, who inherits through his mother, a distant cousin of the Kirkstones. If he died Edith Wedderburn would inherit."

"Who is she? Another cousin?"

"Yes. Even more distant than Alder. She is now at Kirkstone Hall, looking after it for Miss Gilmar, who placed her there. So far as the personal estate is concerned Miss Gilmar can leave it by will to whomsoever she pleases."

"Have you the will?"

"Yes. But I can't open it save in the presence of those likely to inherit: Miss Wedderburn and Alder—in short, the relatives."

"Whom do you think the money is left to?"

"It's not my place to say," said Prain, with sudden stiffness.

Gebb saw that the little solicitor knew the contents of the will, but he was bound by professional etiquette, and could not disclose them.

"Well," he said, covering his disappointment with a cough, "we may leave that out of the question. Tell me about Miss Wedderburn."

"I have told you," replied Prain, sharply. "She is the caretaker of Kirkstone Hall, and is very poor."

"Is she very pretty?"

"Extremely pretty."

"Ho! ho!" said Gebb, in a jocular tone; "in that case she must have lovers."

"She has two," answered Prain, dryly. "One is John Alder."

"What! the heir?"

"Yes! If she marries him she will still be mistress of Kirkstone Hall. But she won't," said Prain, rubbing his chin with a vexed air, "for the simple reason that she likes her other lover better."

"Who is the other lover?"

"An artist called Arthur Ferris. He is poor, but handsome."

"Good looks won't make the pot boil," said Gebb, sententiously. "Well, I'm not particularly anxious for further information about her love affairs. What I wish to know is, if Miss Wedderburn corresponded with Miss Gilmar."

"I can't tell you that: I don't know."

"Do you think Miss Wedderburn is aware of her cousin's death?" said Gebb, putting the question in another form.

"It's improbable, as she would have written to me on the subject had she known. By the way, is the body buried?"

"Of course; it is two weeks since the murder."

"True, I forgot," said Prain, thoughtfully. "I wonder if Alder knows about her death."

"He can't know, unless he traced her by the Yellow Boudoir."

"Oh, Alder doesn't know much about that room and its crime, as he belongs to the younger generation, and the story is almost forgotten. However, I'll write to him on the subject. It is necessary that he should learn his position as speedily as possible, if only on account of the will."

"That is your own concern," said Gebb, rising. "Still you might arrange for me to have an interview with him, as he might throw some light on the subject."

"I fail to see how he can," said Prain, raising his eyebrows. "Miss Gilmar never corresponded with him during her travels. If any one will know about her, it will be Miss Wedderburn."

"Ah! I'm going down to see her," said Gebb, putting on his hat. "I'll have a look at the original of the Yellow Boudoir at the same time."

"I say," said Prain, as the detective moved towards the door.

"Well!" replied Gebb, turning.

"If you see Edith, ask about her lover."

"Which of them, Alder or Ferris?" said Gebb, stolidly.

"Don't mention the name of either," repeated Prain slowly, "but ask about her lover. Then—well, you'll see what will come of your question."

The detective gazed steadily at the solicitor.

"What do you mean?" he demanded, struck by the significance of the man's words and look.

"You'll find that out when she answers."

"How will she answer?" demanded Gebb, quite mystified.

"Ah!" said Prain, with a long breath, "you ask and see."

CHAPTER IX

KIRKSTONE HALL

The day following his conversation with the little solicitor, Gebb left Waterloo Station for Norminster in Hampshire, and arrived at that quaint little town about midday. On making inquiries he learned that Kirkstone Hall was a mile distant, situate amid some woods near the banks of the Avon.

As it was a fine morning, and Gebb was fond of walking, he used his own legs to reach his destination; and after a pleasant stroll through rural lanes, and across flowering meadows, he reached a pair of finely wrought iron gates which stood wide open. The gates themselves were covered with red rust, the lodge beside them was shut up, and the stately avenue, which curved upward between noble oak trees, was overgrown with grass. Even on the threshold, as it were, of the estate, Gebb espied the ruinous economy of the late Miss Gilmar.

On coming in sight of the Hall, he found the hand of Time still more heavily laid upon the works of man. It was a quaint Jacobean building of red brick, set upon a slight rise, and surrounded by stone terraces. From the main body two wings spread to right and left, but the windows of these were all closely shuttered. The hall door was also closed, and—so far as Gebb could see—no smoke curled from the stacks of chimneys. The terraces were grass-grown, the gardens untended and in disorder, and the whole place had a silent, melancholy aspect as though the soul of the house had departed. It was the palace of the Sleeping Beauty, enchanted and spell-bound, and it seemed as though there were a curse on the place.

"And no wonder!" said Gebb, looking at the gaunt mansion, grim even in the sunshine, "seeing the kind of people who lived in it, and the crimes they committed."

He ascended the steps and rang the bell, but before the sound had died away he was aware of a brisk step approaching, and turned to see a young lady walking along the terrace on the right.

She was tall and dark, with fine eyes and a handsome face. Her figure was shown to perfection by the trim, tailor-made costume which she wore. In her hand she carried a silver-headed cane, and walked smartly towards the detective, with the air of a woman fully alive to the importance of time. When she spoke, her voice was deep and full, but the matter of her speech was remarkably business-like.

48

On the whole Gebb judged Miss Edith Wedderburn—for he guessed that this was the young lady referred to by Prain—to be a clever, plain-spoken woman, with few of the weaknesses of her sex to hamper what she conceived to be her duty.

"Good day!" said the lady, with a comprehensive glance. "May I ask what you want?"

"I wish to see Miss Wedderburn."

"Well, you see her now. I am Miss Wedderburn. Can I do anything for you?"

"Yes," replied Gebb, becoming as curt and as business-like as herself, "you can give me a trifle of information."

"Can I?" said Miss Wedderburn, dryly. "That entirely depends upon my humour and what you want to know. Also, why you what to know it. Who are you?"

"My name is Absalom Gebb."

"I am no wiser," interrupted the girl, with pointed insolence.

"Of New Scotland Yard, Detective," finished Gebb, coolly.

This time his reply made a decided impression on his hitherto cool auditor. The rich colouring of her face vanished as by magic, and she became pale even to the lips. Nevertheless, she forced herself to smile with some composure, and controlled her emotion by a powerful effort of will. Startled as she was, she even attempted to speak lightly.

"And what does Mr. Absalom Gebb, Detective, wish with me?" she said in a low voice, her eyes fixed on the man's face.

"He wishes to ask you a few questions," said Gebb in the same vein.

"About what? About whom?"

"About Miss Ligram."

"Ligram! I don't know the name," said Edith, calmly. "Who is Miss Ligram?"

"The owner of this place."

"You are wrong there, Mr. Gebb; the lady who owns this place is called Miss Gilmar."

"I am aware of the fact. But it suited her to take other names while she lived."

"While she lived!" repeated Miss Wedderburn, raising her voice in surprise. "What do you mean?"

"I mean that Miss Gilmar is dead!"

"Dead!"

"Murdered."

"Murdered! Oh, God! When? Where?"

"In a suburb of London called Grangebury on the twenty-fourth of last month."

Edith looked rigidly at the detective with horror in her dark eyes, and for the moment seemed scarcely to comprehend his news. She appeared to be genuinely astonished and shocked; yet her next question conveyed to Gebb a hint that she was not altogether unprepared for the information.

"Did he kill her?" she stammered, laying her hand on Gebb's arm.

"He! Who?" asked the cunning detective, trying to trap her into a hasty speech.

"Dean! Marmaduke Dean!" said the girl, breathlessly.

"What do you know about Marmaduke Dean?"

"Everything! No doubt I know more than you do. Have you never heard of the murder which took place in this house?"

"In the Yellow Boudoir. Yes."

"Ah! you know the story!" cried Miss Wedderburn, suspiciously.

"I do; and I have come down to see you about it. Please take me inside, Miss Wedderburn, and show me the Yellow Boudoir in which Dean murdered your cousin Kirkstone."

"My cousin Kirkstone? You seem to know a great deal of our family history, Mr. Gebb," said Edith, drawing herself up.

"I know as much as a report of the Kirkstone murder could tell me: and as much as Prain the solicitor knows."

"You know Mr. Prain?"

"Yes! I was with him yesterday. But I'll learn no good from this desultory conversation, Miss Wedderburn. Please take me indoors and we can discuss the matter quietly. I am the detective in charge of the case, so you need have no hesitation in telling me all you know."

"I know nothing!" cried Edith, vehemently, "nothing!"

"It is for me to judge of that," retorted Gebb, dryly.

The keen look he gave her, and the significance of his tone and words, seemed to startle the girl. She glanced defiantly at his watchful face, and strove to match his gaze with a steady look of her own; but whether from fear or modesty, her eyes fell, and she turned away to obey his request and lead him within doors. Gebb followed her in silence along the terrace and round the corner of the house, until they both paused before an open French window which led into a pleasant, sunny apartment of no great size. Before entering, Edith, who had evidently been considering his last speech, turned to excuse herself.

"Mr. Gebb," she said, with an air of great dignity, "your words seem to imply that I know more than I dare tell. I assure you that such a suspicion is unjust and unfounded. The intelligence of Miss

Gilmar's death is terrible and unexpected to me; and any aid I can give you to bring the assassin to justice you shall have. Whatever questions you ask me I will answer; whatever you desire to see in this house I will show you; but in justice to myself, I must ask you not to credit me with guilty knowledge."

"My dear young lady, I am the last person in the world to do so," said Gebb, quickly. "I do not for a moment suppose that you know anything of your cousin's unhappy death. I disclaim the sentiments with which you credit me; and I must admit that there is no necessity for you to exculpate yourself as you are doing."

"I am not exculpating myself in the least," rejoined Miss Wedderburn, coldly, "but you detectives seem to be so suspicious that you see ill where none exists."

Gebb laughed. "You have been reading detective novels," said he, indulgently; "believe me, we detectives are not so black as the novelists paint us. But, as I said before, this desultory conversation is not useful. I would rather see the Yellow Boudoir."

Edith nodded, and led the way into the house. Gebb followed her through the sitting-room, which faced the terrace, and down a wide passage, on the wall of which hung many pictures, mostly ancestral portraits. At the end of this passage his guide unlocked a door, with a key selected from a bunch which dangled at her girdle, and threw it open, so that Gebb could pass into the room before her. He did so without hesitation.

"This is the Yellow Boudoir," said Miss Wedderburn, following the detective; "it was in this room that the unfortunate Mr. Kirkstone was killed twenty years ago."

"By Dean!"

"Not by Dean," replied Miss Wedderburn, sharply. "From all I have heard. Dean is as innocent of that crime as you are."

"Then who is guilty?" asked Gebb, artfully.

"I am not a detective," said Edith, moving towards the window, "so I cannot give you an opinion. If you will permit me I will admit air and light so that you can see the room to its fullest advantage."

When they entered, the boudoir had been in a kind of semi-darkness, as the shutters of the one window were closed; but now Miss Wedderburn threw these open, and the sunlight poured in. The dust raised by their feet danced in motes and specs in the sun's rays, and Gebb, dazzled by the strong glare, felt his eyes somewhat painful. However, they soon became habituated to the flood of glorious light, and he looked with deep interest at the original of the room which he had seen in Paradise Row.

The apartment was larger than that which had been occupied by Miss Gilmar in Grangebury, but in every respect the furnishing and appointments were the same, as she had carried out her whim with the utmost care. The furniture, in place of being cane, was Chippendale; the window and door were differently placed; and the colouring of the whole room was more subdued and mellowed by Time. But the predominating hue was the same—the carpet was yellow, sprinkled with bunches of pale primrose flowers, the walls were draped with costly hangings of golden tint, and, from a domed ceiling of drawn silk depended an exact copy of the Arabian lamp studded with knobs of yellow glass. The furniture was cushioned and covered with yellow silk; the vases and metal-work were of brass; there was even a brazen tripod and chafing dish standing in the same position as its imitation had occupied in Paradise Row. The main difference in the room lay in the absence of books, knickknacks, flowers and magazines, which showed that it was not in daily use; otherwise all was the same. Gebb almost fancied that some genii of the lamp had transported the Grangebury palace to Norminster.

"It is just the same," he said aloud, having taken in these details.

"What is the same?" asked Miss Wedderburn, who was standing near the window.

"This room. It is similar to that in which Miss Lig—I mean in which Miss Gilmar was murdered."

The girl looked puzzled. "You are making a mistake," she said. "It was Kirkstone who was killed here, not Miss Gilmar."

"Oh, but I am referring to the room at Grangebury," returned Gebb, quickly.

"Miss Gilmar's lodgings, you mean?" asked Edith, still perplexed.

"Yes. Her room was furnished like this."

"Impossible. From what I knew of my cousin she would not have spent the money in furnishing a costly room."

"Nevertheless she did," replied Gebb, coolly. "Of course the imitation was somewhat gimcrack, and done on a cheap scale; but, for all that, I assure you the resemblance between the original and the copy is marvellous."

"Strange!" muttered Edith, sitting down on a primrose-hued couch. "I wonder why Ellen—— Tell me all about this terrible murder," she broke off; "all—-from the beginning."

CHAPTER X

STRANGE BEHAVIOUR

After some reflection Gebb concluded that Miss Wedderburn was quite ignorant of the causes which had led to her cousin's death; also of the details, and of the death itself. He therefore told her as concisely as possible the story of the tragedy from the time Mrs. Presk had been brought to the Grangebury police-station, down to the visit he had paid to Prain the solicitor. Some points in the story he suppressed, others he amplified; but, on the whole, he gave her a very fair and unprejudiced account.

With attentive ears, and her eyes fixed on the face of the narrator, Edith sat listening, her hands clasped loosely on her lap. Several times she asked him questions, but as a rule let the account flow on uninterruptedly. When Gebb ended, she heaved a deep sigh, whether of relief or pity the detective could not say, and rose to pace up and down the room. Evidently she was more moved by the tragic fate of her wretched cousin than she chose to admit. Gebb having told his story, waited for her to recover, and comment on the matter.

"Poor Ellen!" said Miss Wedderburn at length, but speaking to herself rather than to her companion. "A miserable ending to a miserable life; but I am not astonished."

"How is that?" said Gebb, with a sharp look at her. "Surely the tragedy is unexpected enough."

Miss Wedderburn shook her head. "Ellen always said that sooner or later she would be murdered."

"By Mr. Dean?"

"Yes," replied Edith, quietly, "by Mr. Dean."

"Oh!" said the detective, taking a long breath. "I thought you believed in the innocence of Dean."

"So I do; I never said I didn't. I only remarked that Ellen declared Mr. Dean would kill her."

"Well, she has been murdered, and in the most barbarous manner. Do you say Dean is the criminal?"

"Do you?" said Edith, answering one by asking another.

"I don't know what to think," replied Gebb, crossly.

"Neither do I," responded Miss Wedderburn; and then for quite two minutes there was a dead silence. It was broken by Gebb.

"Was Miss Gilmar unpopular in these parts?" he asked.

"Very unpopular; the people round here called her Mrs. Harpagon, from her miserly habits."

"Did you like her, Miss Wedderburn?"

"No!" replied the girl, coolly, "I did not; neither did she like me. There was no love lost between us. She wanted a caretaker, and I wished for a home. My staying here is a simple matter of business."

"But surely you are sorry to hear of her murder?"

"I am not utterly without heart, Mr. Gebb, although you seem to think so. Yes, I am sorry. I would be sorry for any one who met with so cruel a death."

"Had Miss Gilmar any enemies?" asked Gebb, impatient of this fencing which kept him at a distance.

"I told you she was unpopular," said Edith, slowly, "but I don't know that she had any enemies bitter enough to murder her."

"Except Dean!"

"Of course," she replied unmoved, "always except Mr. Dean."

"Then he must have killed her."

"It's not impossible," retorted Miss Wedderburn, coolly.

Gebb, a rare thing for him to do, lost his temper completely. "Madame!" he cried in a rage, "will you or will you not answer me plainly?"

"There is no need to raise your voice, sir. I am answering you."

"But not plainly!"

"What do you call plainly?" asked Edith, with a provoking smile.

"You know what I mean," said Gebb, testily. "I call black black and white white; you call both a kind of grey."

"I believe they are grey when mixed. However, I see what you mean, Mr. Gebb, so do not lose your temper. You wish to know why Miss Gilmar left this place, how she left it, and why I am in charge."

"Yes, I shall be glad of the information."

"Very good," said Edith, calmly; "then you shall hear my history."

"It will be just as well for you to tell it," said Gebb, dryly; "at least, so far as concerns Miss Gilmar. Every detail is of value in connection with this case. Please go on"—and he took out pencil and pocket-book.

"I am an orphan," said Miss Wedderburn, taking no notice of this action, "as I lost my parents some five years ago. I was then eighteen years of age and at a school in Canterbury, but on the death of my father and mother I was unable to continue my education. Therefore, as I had no parents, no friends, and no money, I was in anything but a pleasant position."

"Did your father leave no money?" inquired Gebb, with sympathy.

"If he had I should not be here, sir. My father died so poor that there was hardly enough money to pay his funeral expenses. I tell you all these details, Mr. Gebb, so that you may understand my position here. When I found myself thrown on the world I did not know what to do, as I was unable to obtain a situation either as companion or governess. Then I remembered Ellen Gilmar—a relative of my father's, who I knew was living a quiet life in this place on the money left to her by Laura Kirkstone. I wrote to her and explained my position; and, as she no doubt found life here extremely dull, she asked me to stay with her as a companion, but without a salary. The offer did not attract me greatly, nor did Ellen on our first interview; but I was in that unenviable position when beggars can't be choosers, so I was forced to accept her offer. I have been here for the last five years, and on the whole I have no reason to complain of my lot in life."

"Was Miss Gilmar kind to you?"

Edith shrugged her shoulders. "As kind as she could be to any one. We quarrelled once or twice."

"About what?"

"I don't see that you have any right to ask that question," said Edith, quietly. "Still, to show you how candid I am, I will answer it frankly. We quarrelled about a certain Mr. Alder."

"What! John Alder the barrister?"

"Yes," said Miss Wedderburn, rather surprised; "do you know him?"

"Not personally; but I heard about him from Mr. Prain."

"Mr. Prain seems to have been very confidential. However, this gentleman wished to marry me, and Miss Gilmar thought that I ought to accept him, as he was the heir to the Kirkstone estates and also because she intended to leave him her money."

"Without a provision for you?"

"Oh," said Miss Wedderburn, indifferently, "Ellen was not bound to leave me her money, seeing that she had provided me with free board and lodging. But she advised me to marry Mr. Alder, and so make certain of being comfortable for life. But I did not like him, so I refused to become his wife. Now I suppose he will turn me out-of-doors."

"Would he be so cruel?" said Gebb, with a glance at her handsome, haughty face.

"He might, and he might not. He is much liked by his friends, and, I suppose, has as much charity as most people; but whatever he

55

decides, I can't stay on here, now that he is the master. Does he know that his cousin is dead?"

"I can't say. I don't think so; unless, like myself and Prain, he discovered her death through the newspaper descriptions of the Yellow Boudoir."

"He'll find out soon, I've no doubt," said Edith, "and come down to offer me a choice of being his wife or leaving the Hall. I shall certainly go. But to continue my story. I remained with Miss Gilmar, and got on fairly well with her. She told me all about the murder, and her fears of being killed by Dean. Often she congratulated herself that he was in prison."

"And what did she do when she heard of his escape?"

"She was beside herself with terror; and, thinking he would come down here to murder her, she determined to leave the Hall. She made all arrangements as regards money with her solicitor, and asked me to take charge of this place. I agreed, and she went away over three years ago. I have never," said Miss Wedderburn, with emphasis, "set eyes on her since."

"Did you know the course of her wanderings?"

"Sometimes, when she wrote to inquire if Dean had made his appearance at the Hall, but as a rule I heard nothing, and knew not where she was. The last time she wrote was about six months ago, but she did not say then where her next resting-place would be, and as she was not inclined to be confidential I did not ask questions."

"Did you know that she carried about a duplicate of this room?"

"No, not until you told me. I never see the newspapers down here."

"Can you tell me why she did so?"

"It is hard to explain," said Edith, with a puzzled look. "When Ellen was here she sat constantly in this room, and seemed greatly attached to it. I do not know why, seeing that it had been the scene of her cousin's murder. But I suppose she wanted to keep the threats of Dean to kill her constantly in mind, and so framed a duplicate of this room, that she might not forget her danger and run the risk of being lulled into a state of dangerous security."

"That would hardly account for her strange fancy for the room," said Gebb, shaking his head.

"I can supply no other reason," answered Edith, reflectively. "Ellen was very eccentric, and one could not always account for her whims."

"She was superstitious?"

"Very! Believed in omens and fortune-tellers and all kinds of rubbish. Yet I fancy she had not always been so weak-minded. It

56

was the dread of a violent death that made her consult these people."

"Did she ever drop any hint about the murder?"

"She dropped no hint, as you call it," said Edith, stiffly, "but told me the whole story very plainly. She quite believed that Dean was guilty."

"Yet she might have killed Kirkstone herself," said Gebb, after a pause.

"That is impossible. She had no reason to do so; and moreover if she had been guilty, she would certainly have betrayed herself to me. It is no use speaking ill of the dead, Mr. Gebb."

"Yet you cannot say that your cousin was a good woman."

"Perhaps not," retorted Miss Wedderburn. "On the other hand, I cannot say that she was a murderess. Well, sir, I have told you all I know, and you see I cannot help you in any way."

"I am not so sure of that," replied Gebb, coolly. "I have not yet closed my examination."

Edith flushed and looked uneasy. "I don't like that word," she said in irritable tones; "it sounds as though I were a criminal in the dock."

"That is a strong way of putting it, Miss Wedderburn. Why not compare yourself to a witness in the witness-box?"

"Oh, call me what you like," cried the girl, rising impatiently, "but let us finish our conversation as quickly as possible. I have told you about Miss Gilmar, about this room, about Mr. Alder; I know nothing more."

"Nothing, Miss Wedderburn? Think again."

"I tell you I know nothing," said Edith, now crimson with rage. "What do you mean by your hints?"

"I mean that you have another lover," remarked Gebb, acting on the advice of Prain, but quite in the dark as to what it would bring forth.

Miss Wedderburn sat down promptly again on the couch as though her limbs refused to support her, and the flush on her face gave place to a deadly pallor. She shook in every limb, as though overcome with terror.

"Arthur!" she faltered. "You know about——" Her voice stopped, and she fell back in a faint.

CHAPTER XI

THE MAD GARDENER

Gebb was not easily surprised, being used by reason of his profession to traffic in mysteries; but the unexpected fainting of Edith at his apparently innocent question perplexed him beyond measure. Of course, the girl had not told him the whole of her history, so no doubt in the portions thus kept back lay the explanation of her violent emotion. Gebb, being ignorant of the cause, was amazed at the result.

"Hullo!" said he, throwing open the window to admit fresh air, "there is something queer about this. Prain hinted that if I asked about her lover I might hear something strange, and her actions speak quite as loud as words. This fainting has some meaning in it. Well, well! I must revive her first and question her afterwards."

This was easier said than done, as there was no restorative of any sort at hand. Miss Wedderburn lay back on the couch motionless and white, the image of death; even the breeze from the open window could not restore her senses. Gebb was about to throw wide open the door, and shout for assistance, when through the window he caught sight of a man crossing the lawn, and immediately hailed him loudly. The man jumped round suddenly as though startled by the call, and after some hesitation moved forward slowly and unwillingly to crane his head into the room. He was a queer old creature, with shaggy white hair and untrimmed beard, and two glittering eyes set so closely together as to give him an uncanny look. He was dressed in a suit of old clothes discoloured and rusty; and, with his elbows on the window-sill, moped and mowed in a smiling vacant way at the detective. At the first near glance Gebb saw that the newcomer was not in his right mind.

"Here, my man," he said, making the best of this doubtful assistant, "bring some water; the lady has fainted."

The man grinned, and turned his eyes towards the white face of Edith. Over his own a shade passed, with the result of altering it from gay to grave. He even looked terrified, and with a kind of hoarse cry, pointed one lean finger at the unconscious girl.

"Is she dead? Did you kill her?" he asked in a harsh whisper.

"No! No!!" replied the detective, soothingly, as he would speak to a child, "she has fainted. Bring some water."

"Kill her!" whispered the man, nodding; "it's a good room to kill people in; we use it for that here. I won't tell. I'd rather see her dead than alive; it's better for her. The grave's the bed for a weary head."

"Hush! Bring the water," cried Gebb, shrinking back from the horrible creature. "Be off with you!"

The madman shrank back in his turn at the peremptory tone of the detective, and vanished with a nod, just as a sigh sounded through the room. The cool draught playing on the forehead of Edith had at length produced its effect, and with a second sigh longer than the first, she opened her eyes, and looked vacantly at Gebb. The detective caught her hand, and slapped it vigorously, whereat the girl sat up with an effort, and her faintness passed away. Still her brain was not quite clear, and she looked languidly at Gebb, as though she were in a dream.

"What did you say?" she asked in a low voice. "Am I—have I—what is it?" and she passed a slow hand across her forehead.

"You fainted, Miss Wedderburn," replied Gebb, softly.

"Yes! I remember! I fainted! You asked about—— Oh, God! I know;" and she covered her eyes with one hand.

Before she could speak again, a harsh, cracked voice was heard singing in the distance:—

> "The raven is the fowl for me,
> He sits upon the gallows tree,
> And bravely, bravely doth he sing,
> In a voice so low and rich:
> While flaunting in a garb of pitch
> The murderer's corpse does gaily swing.
> Ho! Ho! Ha! Ha! He! He! He!
> The raven and the gallows tree."

"Ah!" Miss Wedderburn shivered nervously as this gruesome ditty sounded nearer, and put her fingers in her ears to shut out the singing. "It is Martin with his fearful songs!" said she, softly.

"Martin! And who is Martin?" asked Gebb, amazed at these extraordinary proceedings.

"Martin! Martin! Mad Martin!" croaked the harsh voice; and there at the window stood the crazy man, leering in a fawning manner, and holding a tin basin half full of water. Dipping his hand into this, he sprinkled a few drops towards Edith, singing tunelessly the while:—

> "Weep till tears roll as a flood,
> I baptise thee now with blood."

59

With an exclamation of annoyance Edith rose, and, snatching the basin out of the man's hand, shut the window hurriedly. Martin gave a frightened whimper and slunk away; while his mistress, soaking a handkerchief in the water, bathed her pale face. Gebb, judiciously waiting the development of events, stood quietly by, wondering, but silent.

"Is this a lunatic asylum, Miss Wedderburn?" he asked when she was more composed, and he judged it judicious to recommence the conversation.

"No, of course not!" she replied irritably; "the man is mad, but quite harmless. Martin!—Martin!—I do not know his other name. He is an excellent gardener, and usually quiet enough, although he will sing those gruesome songs all about gallows and murders. To-day—for some reason—he is worse than usual."

"He ought to be placed under restraint," said Gebb, carelessly, for he was too bent on questioning his companion to be distracted by a lunatic. "But this is not to the point. May I ask what caused you to faint, Miss Wedderburn?"

The girl raised her head and directed a steady stare at Gebb. "In my turn, may I ask why you come here to question me?" she said defiantly.

"I thought I explained my errand before," replied the detective, mildly. "I am here to learn—if possible—who killed Miss Gilmar."

"I cannot tell you: I know nothing about it. Until you gave me the news I was not aware even that she was dead."

"Yet you were not so surprised by the information as I expected."

"That can be easily explained, Mr. Gebb," said Edith, wringing out her wet handkerchief. "As I told you before, I knew of my cousin's fears. She was perhaps pursued by Mr. Dean when he escaped from prison, with the avowed intention—it was reported—of killing her. She left her home—as I know—in order to hide from him; but it is possible—I say," she added with emphasis, "it is possible that Dean tracked her down and revenged himself for her conduct of twenty years ago. You wish to learn who killed Miss Gilmar, sir? I tell you I do not know! Mr. Dean, in my opinion, is innocent; but on the face of it, I admit that appearances are against him. Perhaps if you find the man and question him you may arrive at the truth."

"It is not improbable," replied Gebb, coolly; "but we must catch him first. Still, Miss Wedderburn, your opinion of Dean's guilt or innocence does not explain your recent conduct. To put a plain question, miss, 'What made you faint?'"

"That is my business!" said Edith, haughtily, but with averted eyes.

"And mine too. Why should you faint because I ask if you have another lover besides Mr. Alder?"

"I refuse to answer!"

"In that case," observed Gebb, artfully, "there must be something wrong with Arthur."

"How dare you call him Arthur?" flashed out Miss Wedderburn.

"Call who Arthur?" asked Gebb, laying a trap for her hasty tongue.

"Mr. Fer——" She stopped and bit her lip, hesitating, as it would appear, whether to tell the name or not. After a momentary pause she evidently deemed bold speaking the safest policy, for she continued calmly: "After all, there is no reason why I should not tell you his name."

"None in the world, so far as I can see," answered the detective, with a shrug. "I know that his Christian name is Arthur, but what is the surname of your lover, Miss Wedderburn?"

"How do you know that I have a lover?" retorted Edith, answering one question by asking another.

"How do I know that you have two lovers?" corrected Gebb, coolly. "Because you told me about one named Mr. John Alder, and Mr. Prain spoke to me about the other. I came here with a certain amount of knowledge, miss."

"Mr. Prain? What has he to do with it?"

"I don't know. I'm waiting for you to tell me."

Edith clasped her hands together with a restless movement, and walked up and down the room hastily. Suddenly, as though making up her mind to the inevitable, she stopped before the detective.

"Mr. Gebb," she said, clearly and distinctly, "I have no reason to conceal anything in my life. I am engaged to a gentleman named Arthur Ferris, whose occupation is that of an artist. He has nothing to do with the murder of Miss Gilmar—that I swear."

"There is no need to swear," said Gebb, wondering at her vehemence; "but why did you faint when I asked you about him?"

"I thought—I thought you might suspect him," faltered Miss Wedderburn, in a low tone. "I know how suspicious you detectives are. You seem to think that I know more than I tell you; but you are wrong—I do not."

"I suspect neither you nor Mr. Ferris," said Gebb, quietly; "but it was so strange that you should faint at a simple question, that I naturally wished to find out the reason."

"Well, sir, you know it now."

"I know the reason you choose to give," replied Gebb, significantly, "but you will excuse my saying that it is rather a weak one."

"I can give no other."

"You could if you wished."

"Then I refuse to give any other," rejoined Edith, with a frown.

"Quite so," replied Gebb, rising. "Well, there is nothing for it but for me to take my leave—for the present," he added significantly.

"This sudden cessation of Gebb's questions alarmed Edith more than the questions themselves had done, and she looked uneasy. Once or twice she appeared about to speak, but closed her lips again without a word, and conducted Gebb silently out of the house. The detective was rather annoyed by this self-control, as the sole reason of his manœuvre was to make Miss Wedderburn talk. Nine women out of ten would have done so, and have defended themselves with many words; but this girl was evidently the tenth, and knew the value of silence. However, Gebb was too experienced to show his annoyance, and, mentally resolving to question this Sphinx on a future occasion, when she was not so much on her guard, he took his leave with a last warning.

"You ought to have that mad gardener locked up," he said, looking up to Miss Wedderburn as she stood on the terrace, "else there will be another murder in the Yellow Boudoir."

"Oh, Martin is quite harmless," replied Edith, calmly. "I told you so before."

"So harmless, that had he lived in Grangebury I should have suspected him of killing your cousin," responded Gebb, dryly, and forthwith took his departure, considerably puzzled, as well he might be, by the attitude of the young lady. So far she had baffled him completely.

As he walked down the neglected avenue he heard the harsh, cracked voice of Mad Martin piping a tuneless ditty, and shortly afterwards met with the man himself face to face. With his lean, bent form, picturesque rags, and venerable white beard, the man looked like Lear, insane and wretched. When he saw Gebb, the creature stopped singing, and broke into a cackling laugh, which had little mirth in it Gebb—usually self-controlled and careless of impressions—shuddered at that merriment of hell.

"Are you in love with her too?" he asked the detective.

"No," replied Gebb, humouring the man. "Why do you think so?"

"John Alder came here and loved her," said Martin, reflectively. "Arthur Ferris came and loved her. I thought you might be a third.

But you won't win her heart—oh no! Young Arthur has done that. Tall, straight, dark, handsome Arthur, with the mark of Satan on his cheek."

"The mark of Satan!" repeated Gebb, puzzled by this description of Ferris.

"Hist!" cried Martin, with uplifted finger. "He is a wizard and she a witch, and they dance in the Yellow Room when the moon is up. Young Arthur has a red mark on his cheek; Satan baptized him there with blood. Oh, blood! oh, blood!" moaned the wretched creature, "nothing but blood.

> "'A knife for you, and a rope for me,
> And death in the Yellow Room;
> I am alive, and you are dead,
> But each hath gotten a tomb.'"

And with a long, dolorous cry Martin ran up the avenue swinging his arms, leaving Gebb to puzzle out his enigmatic verse as best he could.

CHAPTER XII

THE DIAMOND NECKLACE

Gebb, much to his disgust, returned to Norminster as wise as he had left it. Beyond meeting a lunatic, and interviewing an obstinate young woman, he had spent his time and money to little purpose; and it was with a perplexed brain that he sat down to consider his future movements. In the face of his failure he was at a loss how to act. Miss Wedderburn, with what looked like deliberate intention, only repeated the story he already knew.

Miss Gilmar had confessed to a fear of Dean. She had fled from the Hall on account of that fear; her travels and hidings and extraordinary precautions had been undertaken solely to thwart the revenge of Dean. Gebb was aware of these facts; but there was nothing more in them likely to instruct him. He had, so far, exhausted their capabilities.

"What am I to do?" he asked himself for, say, the fiftieth time. "How am I to act? In which direction am I to move? Miss Wedderburn, without any given reason, says that Dean is innocent. Prain is of the same way of thinking, and so am I. Parge alone seems to believe in Dean's guilt, and I don't agree with him. The man himself may be able to supply evidence to reveal the truth; but where is he to be found?"

Gebb could answer this question no more than he could the others he propounded, and vainly racked his usually inventive brain to settle on some course likely to elucidate the mystery. Finally, after mature reflection, he resolved to call upon Prain, and ask him to explain the meaning of Miss Wedderburn's fainting. The lawyer had told him to ask a certain question, and see what answer it would bring. Well, he had done so; and the answer was that the girl, without any apparent cause, had fainted. Perhaps Prain knew the reason; and since Edith refused to reveal it, his sole course was to question the solicitor. So to Prain the detective went, full of curiosity, two days after his return from the country. The interval had been filled up in attending to business unconnected with the Grangebury mystery; but now Gebb returned to it again, and sought Mr. Prain in the hope of learning something tangible. But his spirits were very low.

"Well, Mr. Gebb," said brisk Mr. Prain, after greetings had passed, "I have not been idle since I saw you last I have sent a description of that necklace to the police. I have informed Mr. Alder of Miss Gilmar's death, and I have received his instructions about the will."

"There is a will, then?"

"Without doubt. Miss Gilmar made her will before she left the Hall."

"In favour of Mr. Alder?" said Gebb.

"Yes. Of course, by the will of Kirkstone's ancestor Mr. Alder becomes possessed of the Hall; but Miss Gilmar has left her personal property—that is, the money which she inherited from Laura Kirkstone—to him also. Miss Wedderburn, I am sorry to say, receives nothing."

"Poor girl. She will have to leave the Hall."

Prain shrugged his shoulders. "That is at her own discretion," he said, coolly. "Mr. Alder is in love with her; so if she marries him-"

"She won't marry him," interrupted Gebb; "she is in love with, and engaged to, Mr. Ferris."

"Ah! she told you about that scamp?"

"She told me very little, Mr. Prain; but she fainted when I mentioned the man under the very general description of a lover."

"She fainted! Hum!" Prain looked so serious and perplexed that Gebb was impelled to question him further touching the matter.

"Why did she faint?" asked the detective, bluntly.

"I don't know—that is, I can't exactly say," stammered the other.

Gebb looked at the solicitor, who in his turn stared at the carpet, the ceiling, at the papers on his desk; anywhere but at his questioner.

"Mr. Prain," he said seriously, "you are not treating me fairly."

"I beg your pardon," said Prain, nervously—and as a rule he was not a nervous man, "I don't see how you make that out."

"I do!" replied Gebb, sharply. "You know the reason of that fainting."

"Perhaps I do; but I am not at liberty to reveal my knowledge. The secret is Miss Wedderburn's."

"Has it anything to do with this murder?"

"No," replied Prain, decisively. "That it has not."

"Then why did you tell me to ask her about Ferris?"

"Because I wanted to be sure of something; and that fainting has enlightened me."

"Can't you tell me more?" cried Gebb, with some indignation.

"No, I cannot," answered Prain, bluntly. "Get Miss Wedderburn's permission, and I will. But even if you did know, the knowledge would be of no use to you."

"Has Miss Wedderburn any theory about this murder?"

"Not that I know of. You saw her last, Mr. Gebb."

"Does she know who killed Miss Gilmar?"

"Why not ask her?" said Prain, evading the question.

"I did; and I can't make out what she means. She says that Dean is innocent, but won't give her reason. Now, Parge declares that Dean is guilty."

"Well, Mr. Gebb, perhaps he is."

"Indeed!" sneered Gebb, who was growing irritated. "Last time I saw you, Mr. Prain, you denied his guilt."

"And I do so now!" cried Prain, warmly. "I believe, as you do, Gebb, that Dean is innocent of both crimes. He killed neither Kirkstone nor Miss Gilmar. I don't know what Miss Wedderburn's reasons are, but she is right to defend Dean. Still," added Prain with a shrug, "I don't deny that many people look on the man as a murderer."

"Does Mr. Alder believe in Dean's guilt—in his double guilt?"

"Yes. He is sure of it. You can ask him for yourself," added Prain, looking at his watch. "He'll be here soon."

"I'll be glad to meet him. But what is your opinion about this crime?"

"I told you the last time I saw you," replied the solicitor. "Miss Gilmar was murdered by one of those fortune-tellers for the sake of her diamonds. Recover that necklace, and you will soon trace the assassin."

"It's not much of an idea," said Gebb, scornfully.

"It's the best I've got, at all events!" retorted Prain, with heat. "I have done my best to prove its truth by sending a description of that necklace to the police."

"I dare say the description is in the hands of all pawnbrokers by this time," said Gebb, thoughtfully. "Well, we shall see what will come of it. What about Ferris?"

"Ferris!" repeated Prain, in no wise astonished at this abrupt question. "Well, he is an artist, and a bit of a scamp, with whom Edith Wedderburn is in love. I don't know why; perhaps because he is a scamp. Women seem to like scamps, for some reason best known to themselves."

"Is he handsome?"

"Very. Tall and dark; rather military-looking."

"Has he a mark on one cheek?"

"Yes, a birth-mark; but not disfiguring. How did you know about it?"

"That lunatic at Kirkstone Hall told me. He called it the mark of Satan. By the way, who is that man?"

"A gardener who used to live at the Hall in Kirkstone's time. I think the tragedy of the Yellow Room must have sent him off his head. At all events, he ran away after it occurred, and only turned up a year or two ago, quite mad."

"Why didn't they lock him up?"

"Well, you see, Miss Wedderburn (who is rather a strong-minded young woman) thinks kindness may cure him; so she gave him back his old post of gardener. If Miss Gilmar had been there, I don't think he would have been allowed to stay. I don't think, either, that Miss W.'s experiment will be a success."

"He sings the most gruesome songs—about murder, and blood, and the Yellow Room."

"I know," replied Prain, cheerfully. "I am afraid that last muddled his brain and inspired his muse. He didn't sing or compose verse when I knew him; but the man's a complete wreck. He used to be rather handsome and stupid; but his own father wouldn't know him now. I'm sorry for the poor devil, as now that Alder owns the Hall I dare say he'll be kicked out, and have to end his days in an asylum."

"The best place for him, in my opinion," said Gebb, emphatically. "He is as mad as a March hare, and not half so harmless. Hullo! Who is that knocking? Come in."

It proved to be a note from Inspector Lackland, asking Gebb to come down to Grangebury. In the first instance it had gone to Scotland Yard, and, as it seemed important, had been sent on to the detective, who had left word that he would be at Prain's, in case he was wanted.

"Seems important," said Gebb, reading it. "I wonder what Lackland wants to see me about—eh, Prain?"

But Prain was not attending to him. He was busy shaking hands with a tall, broad-shouldered man, fair-haired, blue-eyed, and altogether comely to look upon. This gentleman was introduced to Gebb by the name of Alder; whereby the detective was informed that he stood in the presence of Miss Gilmar's heir and Miss Wedderburn's lover. Alder on hearing Gebb's name looked at him keenly, and saluted him with marked cordiality.

"I am glad to meet you, Mr. Gebb," he said, in loud and hearty tones; indeed, he was rather like a fox-hunting squire than a barrister. "How are you getting on with the case of my poor cousin's murder? Have you caught Dean?"

"No," answered Gebb, plainly; "and, to tell you the truth, I am not sure that Dean is the culprit."

"But if you knew what Dean said about——"

"I know all that Dean said," interrupted Gebb, "also that he escaped; but, for all that, I do not think he killed Miss Gilmar—or Kirkstone either, for the matter of that."

"Hum!" said Alder, thoughtfully. "I see you are of Basson's opinion."

"Mr. Clement Basson! Do you know him?" asked the detective.

"I should think so!" replied Alder, smiling. "I have known him for years. He was Dean's counsel in the Kirkstone case."

"I instructed him," said Prain, complacently. "He believed in Dean's innocence as I did; but unfortunately our united efforts could not get the poor devil off."

"I think I'll call on Mr. Basson," said the detective, thoughtfully. "Where is he to be found?"

"No. 40, Blackstone Lane, Fleet Street," replied Alder promptly; "but what do you expect to learn from him?"

"His reasons for believing Dean not guilty."

"They are the same as mine," cried Prain, "and I don't know how his stating them over again can help you. He does not know where Dean is."

"Still Mr. Gebb had better see Basson," suggested Alder, with conviction. "Something may come of the visit. Will you call on me afterwards, Mr. Gebb, and tell me what you learn from Basson? I am to be found in the Temple, and, as you may guess, I am most anxious that Dean should be traced. I intend to offer a reward of two hundred pounds for his capture. I hope you will earn it."

"I hope so, too," answered Gebb, much pleased; "but you are certain that Dean is guilty?"

"If he is not, I don't know who is," replied Alder, emphatically; and for the time being the conversation ended.

Gebb left Alder to consult with Prain as to the necessity of exhuming the body of Miss Gilmar for identification, and took his way down to Grangebury to learn why the bluff Lackland had written so earnest and urgent a note. He found the plethoric inspector in a state of excitement bordering on apoplexy, and wondered what could have occurred to stimulate the martinet to such unusual excitement.

"That you, Gebb?" cried Lackland, the moment the detective put his nose inside the door. "George! I am glad to see you. It's found, sir—found! What do you think of that, hey?"

"What is found? the name of the murderer?"

"No, no; but something as useful. The diamond necklace," said Lackland, slowly.

"You don't say so!" cried Gebb, excitedly. "Was it sold—pawned——?"

"Pawned!" interrupted the inspector. "Aaron and Nathan's,

68

Harold Street, City. It came into their possession the day after the murder."

"The devil! Our assassinating friend lost no time. Who pawned it?"

"A young man who called himself James Brown."

"James Fiddlesticks," said Gebb, contemptuously—"a false name. What was he like?"

"Tall, dark, handsome," said Lackland, with military brevity. "Aaron said that he put the necklace up the spout as cool as a cucumber. He was——"

"Hold on!" cried Gebb, eagerly. "Had he a mark on one cheek—a birth-mark?"

"By George, he had! A purple spot; but not large enough to spoil his looks."

"I thought so!" said the detective, joyously. "So it was Arthur Ferris did it."

"Arthur who?" asked Lackland, gruffly.

"Arthur Ferris, of Chelsea, artist. He pawned the necklace; he stole the diamonds; he murdered Miss Gilmar. Hurrah! we've got him."

CHAPTER XIII

ARTHUR FERRIS

The unexpected discovery that Ferris had pawned the necklace, spurred Gebb to unusual activity. No longer doubtful how to act, he hastened to procure a warrant of arrest against the young man; yet before doing so, and to be certain that his belief was not a false one, he called first at Aaron and Nathan's. These worthy Jews he questioned closely concerning the necklace, and the man who had pawned it. The ornament corresponded in every way with the description furnished by Prain; and the individual, on the evidence of his appearance, and of the birth-mark on his right cheek, could not be mistaken for any one but Ferris. Furthermore, his connection with Edith, who in her turn was connected with the murdered woman, gave colour to Gebb's assumption that Ferris was the guilty person.

"I understand now why Miss Wedderburn fainted," said Gebb to himself. "She thought, when I mentioned him as her lover, that I had discovered the truth, and feared for his safety. No doubt, having informed him about that necklace, and Miss Gilmar's fear of death, he killed and robbed the woman in the hope that Dean would be blamed."

If things were as Gebb surmised, Ferris, in hoping that his crime would be laid to the charge of Dean, displayed an amount of cunning hardly compatible with his disposal of the plunder. He had accomplished the crime so cleverly, and had escaped so mysteriously, that Gebb could not understand why he had pawned the necklace so openly, the very next day, under the obviously false name of James Brown. The rashness nullified his former caution, for he might have guessed that information concerning the jewels would be sent to all pawnshops. As a criminal, Ferris evidently had to learn the A.B.C. of his craft.

"Why did he not wait until the storm blew over before pawning the necklace," murmured Gebb, much perplexed, "or, at least, take the stones out of their setting and sell them separately, either in London, Paris, or Amsterdam? Discovery would have been more difficult in that case. And why did he pawn them so hurriedly unless he intended to leave England? But in that case Edith Wedderburn would have known of his intended departure, and probably would have gone with him. Rum sort of cove he must be."

Gebb in this manner argued the case for and against Ferris, for the young man's conduct displayed such a mixture of caution and rashness as to perplex the detective. Still it was no use, as he well knew, to waste his time in making bricks without straw, when the arrest of the culprit might enable him to gain a frank explanation of these obviously silly actions; so Gebb, on the evidence of the pawning, procured a warrant and proceeded to take Ferris in charge. As a further mark of the man's folly, he had given a wrong name but a right address; and Gebb, proceeding to Chelsea, asked at an Eden Street house for Mr. Brown, only to be told that Mr. Ferris was the sole lodger in it. The naïve simplicity of this novice in crime almost made the detective swear to his innocence on the spot.

"Confound it!" said Gebb, disconcerted by this, "the man has gone about the pawning so openly that I really believe he is guiltless of the crime. Either that or he's a born fool, although even that is doubtful Miss Wedderburn is not the sort of woman to love an idiot, although she does protect one. Seems to me as I'm dealing with a lot of crazy folk."

Ferris chanced to be absent at the time of Gebb's visit, but was expected back every moment; so, on intimating that he wished to see the artist on a matter of importance, and would wait for his return, the detective was shown into the studio. It was a bare apartment of some size, with ample light, but few decorations. Ferris seemed to be rather a hard worker than an artistic dandy, for there were scattered around none of the knickknacks and "bibelots" which many painters love to collect. There was a sprawling clay-figure near a carpeted daïs for the model, specimens of work on the walls, plaster heads and unfinished pictures lying about in disorder, and on the easel, beside a rusty iron stove, a landscape picture in progress of painting. Altogether the studio looked anything but that of a Sybarite, and in no wise accorded with Prain's description of Ferris as a scamp, for scamps as a rule owe their doubtful reputations to their assiduity in gratifying all their tastes, the best and the worst.

"Yet he must have been hard pushed for money to murder that old woman in order to rob her," said Gebb. "So, if he is economical here, I expect he is wasteful in other ways. Hullo! here's a letter on the writing-table with the Norminster postmark. Empty!" he added in disgust, finding no letter inside. "Yet it is from that girl, I am certain. The handwriting is that of a woman. Hum! And yesterday's date, I see by the postmark. She had been writing to warn him. She knows all about the matter. I wish I could find the letter. She's a deep one, that girl, and as sharp as a needle. She wouldn't have bungled the murder as Ferris has done."

With this doubtful tribute of admiration, Gebb calmly proceeded to turn over the papers on the writing-table, and examine the drawers. But he could find no letter from Edith amongst the loose papers, and the drawers proved to be locked, which showed that Ferris was a more cautious man than his conduct in pawning the necklace indicated. How far Gebb would have proceeded with his search, or how successful he would have been, it is hard to say; for just as he was casting his eyes towards a bureau which, he thought, might contain papers likely to illuminate Ferris and his dark ways, the door opened and the man himself entered with a brisk step. He appeared agitated and rather pale, but on the whole composed and business-like.

For a moment or so he did not speak, but looked at Gebb with no very friendly expression of countenance. On his side, the detective scrutinized the face of the newcomer with close attention, to see in what degree he corresponded to the descriptions of Prain and Martin. He beheld a tall and slender man, with an intelligent expression and brilliant black eyes. On his short upper lip there was a small pointed moustache, which gave him a rather military appearance, and on his right cheek a purple mark, the size of a sixpence, but which—his skin being so dark—did not show very conspicuously. He was dressed quietly and in good style, and to all appearance was a man who respected himself too much to indulge in the profligacy with which he was credited by Prain. Gebb was rather favourably impressed by him than otherwise, and could not help regretting his errand.

"I am told you are waiting to see me," said Ferris, civilly. "May I inquire your business?"

"Is your name Arthur Ferris?"

"It is. May I ask what——"

"I arrest you in the Queen's name!" interrupted Gebb, laying one hand on the young man's shoulder, and with the other drawing forth his warrant.

Ferris turned white even to the lips, and leaped back with an exclamation of alarm and surprise. The detective's action seemed to amaze him.

"Arrest me! Why? What for? Who are you?"

"My name is Gebb; I am a detective. Here is my warrant for your arrest, Mr. Ferris, on a charge of murder."

"Murder!" repeated Ferris, much agitated, as was natural. "You accuse me of murder? There is some mistake."

"People in your position always say so," replied Gebb, dryly; "but there is no mistake. You murdered a woman called Gilmar on the twenty-fourth of July last."

72

"It's a lie! I no more murdered Miss Gilmar than you did."

"That has yet to be proved, sir. Here is my warrant, and I have a couple of men outside in case of need. However, I have no desire to make trouble, and if you come along with me quietly, I shall use you civilly. We can drive to the prison in a hansom."

Ferris, who was looking round wildly, as though for some means of escape, started and recoiled at the sound of the ill-omened word.

"To prison!" he echoed hoarsely. "Great God! you would not take me to prison. I am innocent, I tell you. I know nothing of this murder."

"We have evidence to the contrary," said Gebb, quietly; "and I advise you, sir, to hold your tongue. Anything you say now will be used in evidence against you."

"I shall not hold my tongue," said Ferris, with more composure. "There is nothing I can say likely to inculpate me in the matter. I protest against your action. I protest against being treated as a criminal."

"You can protest as much as you like, Mr. Ferris, but you must come with me. You may thank your stars that I have not put the darbies on you. Give me your word not to attempt escape, and we'll walk out arm-in-arm; no one will guess where you are going. You see, I wish to make matters easy for you."

"I shall not try to escape," said the unfortunate young man, proudly, "as I have done nothing wrong. If I must go to prison on this charge, I must; and I thank you, Mr. Gebb, for your civility, but I swear before God that I am innocent of this crime."

With this speech he resumed his hat and walked slowly out of the studio. Gebb followed forthwith, and slipped his arm within that of Ferris, so that the pair seemed to be leaving the house in a friendly way. Two men were waiting at a distance, but on Gebb's nodding to them to intimate that his charge was amenable to reason, they walked off; and shortly afterwards the detective and Ferris got into a hansom. Gebb directed the driver whither to go, and then turned to comfort his companion, for whose despair he felt extremely sorry. Certainly, the young man's conduct did not suggest guilt.

"Cheer up, Mr. Ferris," he said kindly; "if you are innocent you will soon be out of this trouble."

"I don't know how ever I came into it," replied Ferris, disconsolately. "You mean kindly, Mr. Gebb; therefore, in spite of what you say regarding my remarks being used against me, I shall speak freely. I did not know Miss Gilmar at all. I never set eyes on her in my life; and until yesterday I was not aware of her death."

"I see. Miss Wedderburn wrote and informed you of that," said Gebb, coolly.

"What do you know of Miss Wedderburn?" asked Ferris, in surprise.

"I have seen her and spoken with her; and I know from her own lips that she is engaged to you. On your writing-table I saw an envelope with the Norminster postmark and yesterday's date, so I guessed that she wrote to you about Miss Gilmar's death."

"She did! I have no reason to conceal it. But she did not mention that she had conversed with you."

"Perhaps not, Mr. Ferris. She is a young lady who can keep her own counsel."

"She has no secrets that I know of," said Ferris, haughtily.

Gebb shrugged his shoulders. "She has one about you," he said calmly.

"Indeed!" replied the other with sarcasm. "And do you know what it is, Mr. Gebb?"

"I did not know when I saw her, but I know now. Miss Wedderburn is aware that you killed Miss Gilmar."

"Did she say so?" asked Ferris, anxiously.

"No; but I guess that is her secret. You are guilty, you know."

"I swear I am not!" rejoined Ferris, vehemently. "I never saw Miss Gilmar. I did not murder her. I know nothing about the woman."

"Do you know anything about the diamond necklace?"

"The diamond necklace!" stammered Ferris, changing colour, and with a visible start, for this leading question evidently took him by surprise.

"Yes! the necklace you pawned on the twenty-fifth of July to Aaron and Nathan."

"It—it—was—was mine," replied the young man, as clearly as his consternation would let him.

"It was not yours," said Gebb, sharply; "it was Miss Gilmar's. She wore it on the night of the murder, and it was taken from the corpse."

"I did not take it. I did not take it."

"Yet you pawned it."

"Yes, I pawned it, but I swear I did not take it."

"Then how did it come in your possession?"

"I refuse to answer that question," said Ferris, sullenly.

Gebb shrugged his shoulders. "Just as you please," he said; "but the fact of your pawning that necklace is the cause of your arrest. If you can explain——"

"I explain nothing. I intend to keep my business to myself."

"Then you will be in danger of the gallows."

Ferris bit his lip and shuddered. "I am innocent," he said, wonderfully calm considering his position, "but I refuse to state how I became possessed of the necklace."

CHAPTER XIV

A SURPRISING DISCOVERY

The next day Ferris was brought up before the magistrate on the charge of murdering Miss Gilmar. He looked pale and ill, and heard the evidence of his pawning of the necklace in absolute silence. When he was asked to defend himself he refused to utter a word; he declined even to engage a solicitor; so in the face of this conduct there was nothing for it but to commit him for trial. Ferris asked for bail, but his request being refused, he was taken back to prison, still silent. He might have been a stone image for all the information the law got out of him; and every one marvelled at his obstinacy, so dangerous to himself, so inexplicable to others.

Gebb could not understand why he acted in this way, and risked his neck in so obstinate a manner. Certainly Ferris declared himself to be innocent; but he refused to prove the truth of his words, and preserved an impenetrable silence which at once perplexed and provoked the detective. The only reason he could conjecture for the mulish behaviour of the artist was that the evidence against him was too strong for disproval, and that he knew this to be the case.

"Still he might make an effort to save himself," thought Gebb, as he sat meditating in his office, "if only to tell a lie; although I don't quite see what he could say. Mrs. Presk declared that Miss Gilmar wore her jewels on that evening, and when we found the body those jewels were gone. The principal jewel—which is a necklace—was pawned the day after the murder by Arthur Ferris, who knows Miss Wedderburn, who knew Miss Gilmar; and he refuses to state how the necklace came into his possession. If he murdered the woman his possession of the diamonds is easily accounted for: if he is innocent he must have obtained the necklace from the assassin. Therefore, if not guilty himself, he must know who is: that is plain logic."

Logic or not, the result of the argument was very unsatisfactory, and Gebb, in his own mind, was unable to decide either for or against Ferris. He had that morning informed Prain by letter about the artist's committal for trial, and asked him to call at the prison to discover if possible the reason for the strange conduct of Ferris. Also, he requested Prain to call at his office, and tell him the result of the interview. So when his meditations were interrupted by a sharp knock at the door, he quite expected to see the little solicitor enter. In place of Prain, however, he beheld the burly form of John Alder, who appeared to be different from his usual genial self.

"You are no doubt surprised to see me here, Mr. Gebb," he said, when the first greetings had passed, "but I am greatly disturbed about Ferris. He is a friend of mine, you know."

Gebb did not know about the friendship, but he was well aware that Ferris was Alder's favoured rival with Edith Wedderburn, so wondered at the tender-heartedness of the man who was distressed over the removal of an obstacle to his wooing.

"Why are you disturbed?" asked Gebb, rather sceptically. "What makes you worry over Ferris?"

"Because I am sure he is innocent of this murder," replied Alder. "Oh, I heard all about his arrest and committal for trial from Prain, who has gone round to see him. So I thought I would come and tell you that I am convinced of his innocence."

"But he pawned the necklace, Mr. Alder; he admits that he did."

"Then he must have obtained the necklace from some one else."

"That may be, sir," said Gebb, quietly; "but if he did he refuses to say as much. And whosoever gave him the necklace killed Miss Gilmar."

"What defence does he make?" asked Alder, looking puzzled.

"None. He asserts his innocence, but refuses to explain how he became possessed of the necklace. If he can't explain, or won't explain, those diamonds will hang him."

"In what way? I don't quite see how you arrive at that point."

"Miss Gilmar wore the necklace on the night she was killed," explained the detective; "it was gone when we found the body; so by the strongest of circumstantial evidence the assassin must have taken it."

"All this may be true, Mr. Gebb, but it does not prove that poor Ferris is guilty."

"I think it does," replied Gebb, coolly, "seeing that he pawned the necklace in question. If he isn't the principal, he is an accessory before the fact."

"Won't he confess how he became possessed of the diamonds?"

"No, not to me. He refuses to say a word in his own defence."

"Then I tell you what," said Alder, gravely, "this quixotic young man is defending another person; he is shielding the assassin."

"If he is, that shows him to be an accessory either before or after the fact," repeated Gebb. "But who is the person you think he is shielding?"

"Dean! I believe the man killed my cousin."

"Does Mr. Ferris know Dean?" asked Gebb, looking up sharply.

"No. Nor did he know Miss Gilmar, so far as my knowledge

goes," said Alder, with a nod. "Ferris has been a friend of mine for many years, and although for certain reasons we are not very intimate, I am sure he is not guilty of this crime."

"If Ferris did not know Dean, or does not know him, I don't very well see how he can be shielding him!" cried Gebb, irritably. "If you will excuse me saying so, Mr. Alder, I think you are talking sheer nonsense."

"I am sorry you think so," said Alder, stiffly. "Of course I only state that Ferris is not acquainted with Dean, so far as I am aware; but he may know him for all that."

"Why?" asked Gebb, pertinently.

"Because I am certain that Dean is guilty."

"Admitting that he is—which I don't on the strength of the romantic vow—how did Ferris become possessed of the necklace?"

"I don't know. Only Ferris can explain that."

"Well, then, Mr. Alder, he won't explain. So on the face of it he is guilty, and Dean isn't."

"I tell you he is innocent!" said Alder, angrily, "and my friend Mr. Basson can prove it."

"Basson—Clement Basson, the barrister?" said Gebb, with a stare. "Why, what on earth has he got to do with it?"

"He saw Ferris on the night of the murder!"

"Saw him! Where?"

"At Grangebury! In the evening."

"And Miss Gilmar was murdered at Grangebury," said the detective. "Why, that looks as though Ferris was guilty. Your evidence rather condemns than exonerates him."

"Not at all," rejoined Alder, tartly. "I read the evidence of the murder in the daily papers, although I did not know at the time that Miss Ligram was my cousin, Ellen Gilmar."

"Well. What of that?" inquired Gebb, rather puzzled by the irrelevancy of this remark.

"This much. Mrs. Presk and her servant were at a lecture on Dickens in the Grangebury Town Hall."

"I know that."

"Well, Mr. Gebb, that lecture was given by Basson!"

"By Clement Basson, the barrister, who defended Dean twenty years ago?"

"The same! You must know that Basson is a friend of mine," continued Alder, conversationally, "and a barrister, like myself. He is by no means well off, as he is fonder of play than of work. I suggested to him that he should write and deliver a few lectures in order to make money, for he has a fine voice and is an excellent orator. He adopted my suggestion and wrote a lecture on Dickens;

but being nervous, he wished to make an experiment in the suburbs, before attempting to interest a London audience. I suggested that he should deliver it in the Grangebury Town Hall, as I know many people in that suburb. He consented, and delivered the lecture on the twenty-fourth of July, that is, on the very night my cousin was murdered."

"And Mrs. Presk attended the lecture with her servant," reflected Gebb. "Did you know that Miss Gilmar was in Grangebury?"

"I! No! She took lodgings in Paradise Row under the name of Ligram, you know," said Alder. "I had not set eyes on her for years—in fact, not since she left Kirkstone Hall. Out of terror lest she should be killed by Dean, she kept her address secret from all, although I believe she occasionally wrote to Miss Wedderburn on business."

"I know," replied Gebb, with a nod. "But Miss Wedderburn had not heard from your cousin since six months before the murder; so she was not aware of Miss Ligram's—or rather Miss Gilmar's—presence in Grangebury. But what has the lecture to do with Ferris and his innocence?"

"I'm coming to that," said Alder, quietly. "As I had suggested the lecture to Basson, I wished him to have a large audience, so I asked my friends in Grangebury to attend; also I invited some London acquaintances, amongst them Ferris."

"Did Ferris go to the lecture?"

"Yes. I saw him myself at the door, when I spoke a few words to him. He sat in a front row, and Basson—who knows him—told me that he stayed almost to the end of the lecture."

"Oh," said Gebb, meaningly. "Almost to the end!"

"Well, at all events, he stayed until ten o'clock," replied Alder, rather nettled "And as my cousin was killed about that time, Ferris could not have murdered her."

"No! Certainly not So far as I can see, Ferris can prove an alibi. If so, why does he not defend himself in that way?"

Alder shrugged his shoulders. "I can't say; unless he is shielding some one. I suggest Dean, as I really believe that Dean is guilty; but then—so far as I know—Ferris is not acquainted with Dean. Nor is anybody, for the man has not been heard of since he escaped from prison. But you see, Mr. Gebb, that if my cousin was murdered at ten o'clock—and the medical evidence says she was—Ferris, who was in the Grangebury Town Hall at that hour, cannot be guilty."

"I admit that! I shall look into the matter," said Gebb, "and let me tell you, Mr. Alder, that I think very well of you for coming forward with this evidence, as I know that Mr. Ferris is your rival."

"With Miss Wedderburn," said Alder, colouring. "True enough; but for all that I don't want him to be hanged when I know that he is innocent. If Miss Wedderburn marries Ferris I'll just have to put up with it, that's all."

Gebb was about to express further admiration of Alder's conduct when the door opened unexpectedly, and Prain came hurriedly into the room. The little man looked worried, and with a nod to his brother lawyer, he threw himself into a chair near the detective's desk.

"Well, Gebb," he said, in a vexed tone, "I have been to see that young ass, and I can't induce him to speak."

"There will be no need for it," said Gebb, quietly; "I know now that he is innocent, Mr. Prain."

"How is that?" asked the solicitor, in amazement. Whereat Gebb, with the assistance of Alder, told him of the presence of Ferris in the Town Hall at the hour the murder was committed. Prain was more amazed than ever. "Great Heavens!" he said; "if the man is innocent, and can prove it, as you say, why doesn't he speak out?"

"Because he is screening some one, I think," said Gebb.

"I know he is," said Alder; "and I believe that the some one is Dean."

"Why?" asked Prain, with a sharp look.

"I believe that Dean committed the crime, Mr. Prain."

"Yes, but you also believe that Ferris does not know Dean," cried Gebb, crossly; "so why should he shield him?"

"That is a paradox," said Alder, smiling.

Prain looked up with a grave expression on his face. "It is a paradox which I can explain," he said shortly. "Ferris does know Dean."

"He does know Dean!" cried both his hearers in amazement.

"Yes! I may as well tell you both, that Arthur Ferris is the son of Marmaduke Dean."

CHAPTER XV

THE REVELATION OF MR. PRAIN

"Arthur Ferris the son of Dean!" repeated Gebb, looking alternately at solicitor and barrister. "Well, I never heard of such a thing. Did you know of it, Mr. Alder?"

Alder shook his head with unqualified amazement. "Not I!" he said. "I suggested that Ferris was shielding Dean, only because I am certain Dean is the assassin; and only the assassin could have given that necklace taken from the dead woman to Ferris, but I had no idea that there was any relationship or even acquaintance between them."

"Nevertheless it is true," replied Prain, with a nod. "I was Dean's lawyer, as you know, and he told me much of his family history. When his wife died, he placed his son Arthur with some of her relatives, and went himself as a bachelor down to the Hall, to court Laura Kirkstone for his second wife and meet with his fate. When he was imprisoned for the murder of Kirkstone, the relatives of Arthur gave him his mother's name of Ferris. I have kept my eye on that young man all my life—or, rather, all his life of twenty-five years, and have even assisted him on occasions with money. He is the son of Dean right enough, although he still keeps to the name of Ferris."

"Oh! he knows who he is, then?" said Gebb, sharply.

"Certainly! He has known it for many years."

"Has he any idea of the whereabouts of his father?" questioned Alder.

"No; he would have told me if he had, as he is well aware that I consider his father innocent, and would not give him up to the law even if I knew of his hiding-place."

"Do you believe that Dean is innocent in this instance, Mr. Prain?"

The little man moved restlessly and evaded a direct reply to the inquiry of Alder. "That is a question I cannot answer," he said dubiously. "I asked Ferris if he obtained the necklace from his father, but he denied that he did, and added that he was ignorant of his father's whereabouts. He declared that he had not seen his father since he was five years of age."

"Oh, of course he would say all that!" cried Alder, with scorn, "in order to shield his father, as I suggested; although until you

81

spoke I did not know who Dean really was. The evidence against Dean seems clear enough to me."

"In what way?" asked Gebb, anxious to hear Alder's ground of accusation, since he appeared so certain of Dean's guilt.

"In every way," retorted the barrister. "Dean hunted Miss Gilmar down and killed her in Paradise Row. Being hard up, as he must be, seeing that he is an outlaw and in hiding, he stole the jewels she wore. He, no doubt, gave the necklace to Ferris, as I know the young man is as poor as a church mouse, and kept the other jewels to himself. I don't say that Ferris knew at the time his father had killed Miss Gilmar, but when Mr. Gebb here stated that the necklace was taken from her dead body, Ferris is quick enough to put two and two together, and guess what his father had done. He therefore holds his tongue and refuses to say from whom he got the necklace. A man with his life in jeopardy would not keep silent without a strong motive, and what stronger motive can Ferris have than one which concerns the safety of his father? To me the affair is as clear as day."

"Your case is very ingeniously constructed, I admit," said Prain, dryly, "and you argue the rope round Dean's neck in fine style. Nevertheless your theory is—theory, and nothing more."

"Well," said Alder, with a shrug, "what does Mr. Gebb say?"

"Mr. Gebb says nothing at present," rejoined that gentleman, after a moment's thought. "Least said, soonest mended. When I gather more evidence I shall speak more freely."

"Where do you intend to look for evidence?"

"At Kirkstone Hall. I shall ask Miss Wedderburn why she fainted on the occasion of my mentioning about Ferris; although I did ask her once, and she lied."

"I can explain that," observed Prain, quickly. "I said I would not do so without the young lady's permission, but as I have been forced to tell you about Dean's relationship to Ferris, I may as well reveal the rest. Miss Wedderburn knows that Arthur is the son of Dean, so when you asked her about him, I dare say the thought struck her that you knew of it through me, and intended to accuse him of killing Miss Gilmar to avenge his father. With a revulsion of feeling she fainted. There—you have the explanation from my point of view."

"That's all very well, Mr. Prain; but I wish to have the explanation from Miss Wedderburn's point of view. Where is she now?"

"Still at the Hall," said Alder, gloomily; "but she intends to leave it, now that I am master there."

"Oh!" said Prain, with a smile. "She refuses to be its mistress?"

"Yes! I don't mind confessing it. She is infatuated with Ferris, and when I went down the other day to ask her for the last time to be my wife, she refused me, and declared that she intended to marry Ferris. But I don't bear him any ill-will," said Alder, generously. "We both love Miss Wedderburn, and she prefers him in his poverty to me with my money. Still, I don't know how she can bear the idea of marrying the son of a murderer."

"Perhaps, like myself, she believes in Dean's innocence," said Prain, dryly.

"If he is guilty of the first crime, he is guilty of the second."

"Well," said Gebb, thoughtfully, "there is something in that. Unless Dean had been guilty of Kirkstone's murder, he would not have been so bent upon punishing the woman who accused him of it, and it is just possible he murdered her out of revenge. However, I believe myself that Dean is innocent of both crimes. As to the second, I shall see Ferris again, and try to learn if he got the necklace from his father; as to the first," added Gebb, emphatically, "I shall search Kirkstone Hall for Miss Gilmar's confession."

"Her confession!" repeated Alder, surprised. "What confession?"

"Ah!" said Prain, taking no notice of the barrister's question, and addressing Gebb, "so you are coming round to my opinion—that Miss Gilmar killed Kirkstone."

"It has been my opinion for some time," rejoined Gebb, coolly, "and I believe that Miss Gilmar left a confession behind her telling the truth. I don't think she would risk its discovery by carrying it about with her, so it is probable she wrote it out and concealed it in some hiding-place at Kirkstone Hall."

"In that case search the Hall," said Alder, disbelievingly. "You have my full permission to do so."

"I shall certainly avail myself of it, Mr. Alder. So Miss Wedderburn leaves the Hall. What about her protégé, Martin?"

"That lunatic! I don't know. He had better stay where he is for the present, although I think myself he should be locked up."

"What does Miss Wedderburn think?"

"She says he is mad, but not dangerous, and asked me to let him stay on at the Hall until she is settled—with Ferris, I suppose—when she will take him with her. A nice companion he will be to a young married couple."

"I'm afraid that marriage won't take place for some time," said Prain, gloomily; "even if Arthur does escape, he's too poor to keep a wife."

"In that case," said Alder, rising to take his leave, "there may be a chance for me. While there is life there's hope, you know."

Prain shook his head with a doubtful smile. "While Arthur Ferris lives Miss Wedderburn won't marry you," he said positively.

Alder stopped at the door and looked back. "See here, Mr. Prain," he remarked earnestly, "I'm all fair, square, and above-board. Gebb here will tell you that before you came I defended Ferris, because I consider him innocent. But I believe that his father killed Kirkstone and my cousin, and I am certain that both crimes will be brought home to him. In that case I have my doubts as to whether a proud girl like Edith will marry the son of a murderer. If she does not, she will accept me, of that I am certain; and I shall do everything to bring such a marriage about."

"Well," said Prain, "I've known Edith all her life, and I don't think she will marry you."

"We'll see about that," rejoined Alder, confidently, and swung out of the door with a look of determination in his blue eyes.

Prain shook his head and shrugged his shoulders, for he thought that the barrister was over-confident for a lover. Then he took up his hat to go, and addressed a last question to Gebb.

"Well, sir," said he, grimly, "and what do you intend to do now?"

"Three things, Mr. Prain, and I don't mind telling you what they are. I intend to question both Ferris and Miss Wedderburn, I intend to search Kirkstone Hall for that confession of Miss Gilmar's, which I really believe exists, and I intend to call upon Mr. Clement Basson."

"What about Basson—can he prove anything?"

"He can prove an alibi in favour of Ferris," said Gebb; and forthwith related to Prain all that he had been told by Alder regarding the lecture in the Grangebury Town Hall.

Prain listened attentively, and nodded his head approvingly, for he was pleased to find a loophole for Arthur's escape.

"Very creditable to Alder," he said, when the detective finished. "His conduct in speaking up for Ferris deserves our praise. Few men would be so generous to their rival. But if this is so, why did not Ferris clear himself before the magistrate? He would be free now, had he done so."

"Well," said Gebb, thoughtfully, "so far as that goes, we come back to Mr. Alder's belief. Ferris is shielding his father."

"If he is," said Prain, "Dean must be guilty."

"It looks like it. But I tell you what, Mr. Prain," cried Gebb, emphatically, "as sure as I sit here Dean is innocent! Whosoever killed Miss Gilmar was expected by her; was a friend with whom she was at her ease; that is proved by the smoking and the wine. She would not have been at ease with Dean."

"He might have been disguised as a fortune-teller," suggested Prain.

"No, I don't believe it. No disguise could have hidden him from the eyes of a woman who feared him so. Whosoever killed that woman, it wasn't Dean."

"Then why is Ferris shielding Dean?"

"We don't know if he is; you, yourself, said that he denied it."

"I know I did; I know he does!" cried Prain, in despair. "God bless my soul, what a case this is! The more we talk about it the more confused does it become. I tell you what, Gebb, your only chance of arriving at the truth lies in either forcing Ferris to confess where he got the necklace, or in hunting down Dean."

"I'll try the first of your suggestions at once," said Gebb, putting on his hat. "And if Ferris won't confess to me, I'll write and ask Miss Wedderburn to come to town."

"What good can she do?"

"She can make him confess the truth. What the man won't do for justice he may do for love. However, I'll see him at once. Justice will make the first attempt—Love the second."

"And both will fail!" cried Prain. "You'd better catch Dean, my good man."

"That's easier said than done," retorted Gebb; and the two parted, each more or less exasperated. And very naturally, for the perplexities of the Grangebury murder case were enough to anger the mildest natures, and those of Prain and Gebb were rather the reverse.

Irritated and puzzled by the complexion of affairs, Gebb did not let the grass grow under his feet, but at once visited the prison in which Arthur Ferris was confined. He easily obtained permission to see him and entered to find the young man looking ill and worn, but as firm as ever in his policy of silence, Gebb came to the reason of his visit forthwith.

"Well, Mr. Ferris, you are a nice gentleman to stay here, when a word from you in the Court would clear you of all this."

"What word?" asked Ferris, suspecting a snare, and speaking cautiously.

"Why! word where you were at the time of the murder. I know you did not kill Miss Gilmar."

"How do you know that?" asked the young man, with a start.

"Because you were in the Grangebury Town Hall listening to the lecture on Dickens," replied Gebb. "Mr. Alder told me."

"It is very kind of Alder to defend me," replied Ferris, frankly, "Yes, Mr. Gebb, it is quite true. I was not near Miss Gilmar on that night. I am innocent."

"Then why didn't you say so?"

"I did, several times."

"But why don't you produce your alibi?"

"Because I don't choose to," retorted Ferris, slowly, and turned sulky again.

"So you are shielding your father, after all?"

"Who told you about my father?" he asked tremulously.

"Mr. Prain," said Gebb. "Your father is Dean, who swore to kill that woman for accusing him of Kirkstone's murder. He escaped and killed her and gave you the necklace, and you won't speak because you want to save your father's neck."

"My father has nothing to do with it, Mr. Gebb. I did not get the necklace from him. I don't know where he is. This is my last word," said Ferris, firmly. And it was.

Gebb begged and implored and threatened, but to no purpose. Whatever Ferris knew he kept to himself.

CHAPTER XVI

MISS WEDDERBURN

Having failed with Ferris, owing to the artist's obstinate refusal to speak, Gebb thought that he would hear what Basson had to say. He knew from Prain that the barrister had defended Marmaduke Dean, and although he had not succeeded in obtaining an acquittal, believed that his client was innocent. Dean, of course, must have known that his counsel held this opinion; so, on escaping from prison, with a desire to prove his innocence, it was not unlikely that he might have called secretly on Basson, and implored his assistance. If so, Basson might know a good deal about the man, if he could only be induced to speak out, and it was to gain his confidence in this matter that Gebb paid him a visit.

"Of course hè may know nothing," thought Gebb, as he walked the next day towards Blackstone Lane, in which Mr. Basson— according to Alder—had his abode. "On the other hand, if Dean called on him, which is not unlikely, he may know a good deal. I wish to learn where Dean is hiding; how he manages to live; and what his movements were towards the end of July last. Basson may be able to inform me of these matters If he can, so much the better; if he can't, I'll go down to Kirkstone Hall to search for that confession, and see Miss Wedderburn before she leaves the place. If she can't force Ferris to speak, no one else can; the man is as obstinate as a pig."

With this elegant simile Gebb turned out of Fleet Street into Blackstone Lane, and shortly found himself climbing the narrow staircase of No. 40. Mr. Basson being poor and briefless, and evidently careless of his ease, lived at the very top of the high building. After ascending four flights of steep stairs, the detective came upon a door with the name "Clement Basson" painted on it in black letters. Also there was a dingy scrap of paper, on which was written, "Back in five minutes"; so it seemed, much to Gebb's disappointment, as though Basson were not in his office. However, two or three sharp knocks brought forth a grinning boy in a suit several sizes too small for him, and this lad, having put Gebb through a short examination, with the intention of discovering if he had a bill or a writ, or a judgment summons in his pocket, at length relented, and announced that Mr. Basson was within. Evidently the "Back in five minutes" label was used to beguile creditors into thinking that Mr. Basson was absent. That announcement, and the conversation with the juvenile Cerberus, gave Gebb an immediate insight into the state of Mr. Basson's finances, and his Bohemian mode of hand-to-mouth living.

Shortly he was ushered into a dingy chamber, very barely furnished, and very dirty. There was a yellow blind pulled up askew on an unclean window; below this a deal table covered with green baize, ink-stained and worn-out, which was piled up with dirty papers. An ancient bookcase, with a brass screen, was filled with an array of untidy-looking volumes in calf-skin, with red labels; there were two chairs—one for the lawyer and one for any possible client, a rusty grate, filled with torn-up papers, and an empty Japan coal-scuttle. In the midst of these ruins of prosperity, like Marius amid the remains of Carthage, sat Clement Basson, a tall, jovial-looking man, with a fine head of grey hair, a quick eye, and a neatly trimmed beard and moustache. He was carelessly dressed in a kind of sporting fashion, and wore an old cricketing-cap on the back of his head. The man was clever, kindly, and quick-witted; he was also thriftless, weak-willed, and untidy. His worser qualities weighed down his better; and with many qualifications for climbing to the top of the tree, Mr. Basson preferred, out of sheer idleness and lack of concentration, to dance gaily round the trunk in ragged attire. He looked like a survival of Grub Street; one of the feather-headed crew who wrote pamphlets and starved in garrets, and naturally belong to the reigns of the early Georges. He was quite out of place in the late Victorian epoch—an ironical survival of the unfittest.

"Good day!" he said, in a rich baritone voice, advancing to meet his visitor. "What can I do for you, Mr. Gabb?"

"Gebb, sir; not Gabb," answered the detective, seating himself in the one other chair.

"The boy said Gabb," retorted Basson, returning to his chair. "He was thinking of his own gift, maybe;" and he laughed heartily at his rather feeble joke. "Well, Mr. Gebb, have you brought me a brief?"

"No," said Gebb, smiling, for the man's good humour was infectious. "I'm in a different branch of the law to a solicitor. I don't deal in briefs so much as in handcuffs."

"Ah! You are a detective. A Bow Street Runner."

"Yes. In charge of the Grangebury murder case."

"Just so!" said Basson, with a nod, and looking grave. "I read about it in the papers; and now I remember, your name was mentioned. Well, and have you caught the blackguard who murdered the poor woman?"

"Not yet I've come to see if you can help me."

"I?" said Basson, much amused. "You've come to the wrong shop, then. How should I know the assassin?"

"If I can believe Mr. Alder, you knew him once," was Gebb's reply.

"Ah! So Alder has been speaking to you about me. He thinks that Dean is guilty, and I was Dean's counsel in that Kirkstone case. Is it that you are driving at, Mr. Gebb?"

"It just is. Do you believe that Dean is guilty?"

Basson did not reply immediately. He lighted a German pipe of porcelain, and, blowing out the match, placed it in a little pile which lay near the inkstand. Then he puffed out a cloud of smoke, and through it looked at his visitor.

"Why do you ask me?" he demanded abruptly.

"I want your opinion. I know from Mr. Alder that you did not believe Dean guilty of Kirkstone's murder."

"No. That I did not," rejoined Basson, hastily. "No more than I believe Mr. Ferris—poor boy—guilty of this one. I was coming to tell you that he was at my lecture on the night of the murder, but Alder said he would speak to you about it. Did he?"

Gebb nodded. "I know that Ferris is innocent, but he had the necklace in his possession, and that is a suspicious circumstance."

"I saw about that in the papers," said Basson, nodding. "Well, and how does he say the necklace came into his hands?"

"He declines to tell me."

"Does he? With his neck in the noose, so to speak."

"Precisely, Mr. Basson; he did not even confess his presence at your lecture. He said he was innocent, and for the rest held his tongue."

Basson stared, and pressed the tobacco in the pipe bowl with his little finger. "Now, that's queer," he said. "Why does he act in this way?"

"I think he wishes to shield his father."

"I didn't know he had a father. Thought his father was dead."

"As good as dead, I am afraid. Dean is his father."

"What!" Basson's pipe fell out of his hands, and he looked at Gebb in amazement. "Dean, the man I defended, Ferris's father?"

"Yes, Ferris lived with some relations, who changed his name when his father was condemned. Now, Mr. Basson, I don't believe Dean is guilty of this second murder; but on no other ground than that he did kill the woman, and gave Ferris the necklace to pawn, can I account for the young man's silence."

"Does he say that Dean is guilty?" asked Basson, picking up his pipe.

"No; he denies it, but refuses to confess how he became

possessed of the necklace. Mr. Basson, tell me on what grounds you believed that Dean did not kill Kirkstone."

"No motive," rejoined Basson. "People don't commit murders without motives. But a year or two ago I got an anonymous letter, which strengthened my belief in his innocence. Wait a bit, and I'll get it for you."

He opened a small safe standing at the end of the room near the bookcase, and after five minutes' groping in its depths, at length fished out a dingy bit of paper, which he brought back to Gebb. This he spread out on the table, and raised his finger to enforce the attention of the detective.

"Dean declared his innocence to me," said the barrister, with forensic force, "and I believed him. But he thought that Laura Kirkstone was guilty—that in a mad fit she killed her brother. I did not agree with this, for I held then, and I hold still, that Ellen Gilmar stole that knife from Laura, and murdered Kirkstone before she went upstairs to call Dean and inculpate him in the murder. Now, when Dean escaped from prison I received this letter; read it."

Gebb glanced his eye rapidly over the scrap of paper, which contained two lines of writing running thus: "If you see Dean, tell him not to hunt down a wretched woman. When she dies justice shall be done." To this there was no name and no date and no envelope. Gebb inquired after this latter.

"I'm sorry to say I destroyed it by mistake," said Basson, with regret; "but I remember that it had the Norminster postmark on it, therefore I am sure the note came from Miss Gilmar."

"But why should she write to you?" inquired the detective.

"She fancied Dean on escaping might visit me to get my aid to prove his innocence."

"I thought such might be the case myself," said Gebb, thoughtfully, "Did he come near you at any time after his escape?"

"No," said Basson, emphatically, "I never saw him from the time he went into prison. I don't know where he is; I wish I did, as this note shows that Miss Gilmar knows herself to be guilty, and has left some sort of confession behind, to be read after her death and clear Dean."

"Where do you think this confession is to be found?"

"I don't know. She may have hidden it in Kirkstone Hall, or may have had it with her. When I got this note I went at once to the Hall to tax Miss Gilmar with writing it. However, she had fled out of fear of Dean, and I could not learn her whereabouts. The next I heard was her murder at Grangebury under the name of Ligram."

"Do you think Dean' killed her?" asked Gebb, anxiously.

"I don't know. He might have found her and tried to force her

90

into confession, and failing getting her to do so have killed her; but I don't know."

"Well," said Gebb, getting on his legs, "I had an idea myself that there might be a confession concealed in Kirkstone Hall. Now, on the evidence of this note, I am sure of it. I'll go down and search. But tell me frankly, Mr. Basson, do you know where Dean is to be found?"

"No," said Basson, solemnly, "I swear I don't."

"I must rely on myself, then," said Gebb, with a sigh. "I'll see you again, Mr. Basson."

"I shall be glad to help you, sir," replied the barrister, and bowed the detective out of his dingy room.

Gebb retired in an exultant frame of mind, as he had discovered beyond all doubt that a confession by Miss Gilmar was in existence which would probably exonerate Dean from all complicity in Kirkstone's murder. The question was, where to search for it. On his way back to the office Gebb tried vainly to find an answer to this query, but it was banished from his mind when he discovered that no less a person than Miss Wedderburn was waiting to see him. She approached him at once when he entered, and there was a sparkle of rage in her eyes, which intimated that the object of her visit was not a peaceful one.

"Here you are at last, Mr. Gebb!" she said, in a wrathful voice. "And pray, sir, what do you mean by arresting Mr. Ferris?"

"Oh, that's your trouble, is it, miss?" answered Gebb, coolly. "Well, my dear young lady, I arrested Mr. Ferris because he pawned a diamond necklace!"

"And what had that to do with you, may I ask?"

"This much, miss. The necklace was the property of Miss Gilmar, and was removed from her dead body."

"Nothing of the sort!" cried Edith, vehemently. "Ellen was alive when she gave away that necklace."

"Gave away that necklace!" repeated Gebb, starting up. "What do you mean?"

"What I say!" rejoined Miss Wedderburn, tartly, "I gave the necklace to Arthur, and it was Miss Gilmar who presented it to me in Paradise Row, on the night she was murdered."

CHAPTER XVII

AN EXPLANATION

It took Gebb some time to grasp the meaning of Miss Wedderburn's remarks, for the information it conveyed seemed impossible of belief. He looked so doubtful, that she repeated her speech with some impatience.

"I tell you Miss Gilmar gave me that necklace on the night she was murdered."

"At what hour?" gasped Gebb, not quite master of himself.

"Shortly after nine o'clock."

"Did you see her on that night?"

"Of course I did!" said Edith, sharply. "How else could I have got the necklace?"

"But you told me at Kirkstone Hall that you did not know Miss Gilmar was in Grangebury."

"That is perfectly true," rejoined Edith, colouring; "but I told you many things that were false. I was forced to do so, to protect Arthur and myself."

"So you knew of the murder when I paid my first visit?"

"Yes; and when you inquired after Arthur, I fancied you had discovered his pawning of the necklace, and that you intended to accuse him of the crime. Naturally, I was anxious to save him."

"That was why you fainted," said Gebb, suddenly enlightened.

"It was. In a moment I saw Arthur's danger, as I knew well he would not say that I gave him the necklace; so the thought made me faint. When I learned later that you knew nothing, I held my tongue."

"You did, and to some purpose. I congratulate you on your power of acting, Miss Wedderburn. You deceived me completely."

"What else was I to do?" said Edith, resentfully. "You would not have had me betray myself or Arthur? How did you find out that the necklace was pawned?"

"That I shall explain later," replied Gebb, annoyed by her attitude. "And, in my turn, may I ask why you killed Miss Gilmar?"

Edith stared at him in surprise, and laughed. "You are making a mistake!" she said with haughty coolness. "I did not kill Ellen Gilmar."

"But you were with her on that night?"

"So I was; but I left her at nine o'clock, and then she was alive and well. Why should I kill her?"

"To obtain the necklace."

"What nonsense you talk, Mr. Gebb. She gave me the necklace for Arthur, of her own free will. Even if she had refused to give it to me I should certainly not have murdered her. I love Arthur very much, it is true, but hardly enough to commit so wicked a deed for his sake."

"Do you swear that you are innocent?" asked Gebb, looking at her keenly.

"Yes, I swear I am," she answered, meeting his look with much frankness. "If necessary I can prove my innocence, and that of Arthur."

"Oh, Mr. Alder has proved his innocence already."

"Very kind of him," said Edith, with sarcasm, "for I dare say he was glad enough to hear of Arthur's arrest."

"You do him wrong, Miss Wedderburn. On seeing the case in the paper Mr. Alder came round at once to see me. He stated that Mr. Ferris was present in the Town Hall at Mr. Basson's lecture, and therefore could not have been with Miss Gilmar at ten o'clock, the hour when she was killed. He proved your lover's innocence."

Edith raised her eyebrows and looked surprised. "Why did Mr. Alder do that?" she said, half to herself. "He hates Arthur because—"

"Because he is engaged to you," finished Gebb. "That is a mistake, miss; for Mr. Alder is quite friendly with Mr. Ferris, and bears him no grudge for winning your hand. You may not credit it, but Mr. Alder is a real gentleman."

"The leopard can change his spots, then," said Edith, still puzzled. "I should never have thought that Mr. Alder was so generous. It is very strange," she finished musingly—"very strange indeed."

The detective quite agreed with her. He thought that the whole affair was wonderfully strange, particularly as he was ignorant of how Edith had obtained a valuable necklace from an old miser like Miss Gilmar; and, also, he could not understand her reason for taking it. He quite saw that she had deceived him in order to save herself and Ferris from being accused of the murder, but he was doubtful if she was so innocent of all knowledge concerning the death as she feigned to be. With this idea in his mind he addressed her with some sharpness, and asked her a leading question.

"If you did not kill the woman yourself," said he, "who did?"

"I don't know," answered Edith, candidly. "She was alive when I left her at nine o'clock, and when I saw her death in the paper I was as much surprised as any one."

"You knew, then, that she called herself Miss Ligram at Grangebury?"

"Oh yes, else I would not have known she was the victim. Though, to be sure," added Edith, with a nod, "the description of the Yellow Boudoir would have made me suspect. I spoke falsely for my own ends when I told you that I saw no newspapers at Norminster."

"Well, Miss Wedderburn," said Gebb, after a pause, "I see no reason to doubt your innocence, but I should like to hear your reasons for getting the necklace."

"I'll tell you the whole story, Mr. Gebb. Indeed, I am sorry now that I did not do so when you called to see me; but I was afraid of getting Arthur into trouble, and so held my tongue."

"It was your silence which caused his arrest," said Gebb. "Had you spoken out, he would not have been arrested."

"He could have exculpated himself," protested Edith, earnestly.

"I dare say; but in order to shield you—as I now see—he refused to speak. However, we can talk of these things later, Miss Wedderburn. Tell me your story."

"Certainly; I shall explain fully," said the girl, quickly, "and anything you do not quite understand you can ask me about afterwards. Well, Mr. Gebb, you must know, first of all, that Arthur is the son of Marmaduke Dean, who——"

"I am aware of that fact," interrupted Gebb. "Prain told me."

"Very good," said Edith, composedly. "It makes my task the easier. Yes, he is the son of Dean; and when his father escaped from prison, some years ago, he came down to Kirkstone Hall to see if the poor man had returned there. You know that Dean desired to revenge himself on Miss Gilmar for her share in his condemnation. Well, Arthur thought that his father might have gone to the Hall to punish her; so he came down to warn Miss Gilmar and prevent a second crime, if possible."

"And what did Miss Gilmar do?"

"She was greatly alarmed by the news; and, terrified lest Dean should really come, she went away, as I told you before, and hid herself in London under those several names. It was in this way that I became acquainted with Arthur, and we were very friendly. He used to visit me frequently, and in the end we fell in love with one another."

"As was natural," said Gebb, smiling. "But before you proceed, tell me if Dean ever came to the Hall, as he was expected."

"No," replied Edith, vehemently, "he never did. I don't know where he is."

"Does Ferris know?" asked the detective, eagerly.

"Not he! Neither of us have set eyes on his father. The poor man may be dead for all we know."

"I'm not so sure of that," said Gebb, thinking of the murder. "Go on, please."

"I would not tell you about my engagement," said Edith, who did not relish the smiles of the detective, and therefore spoke with some resentment, "but that it is necessary for the safety of Arthur and myself that I should speak freely. Mr. Ferris"—she adopted this more formal style of mention to keep Gebb in order—"Mr. Ferris came to see me frequently, and confided to me all his troubles. He was greatly in want of money, as his pictures did not sell, and he had no one to help him. I could not, as I had no money, and I was simply earning my living as my cousin's housekeeper at Kirkstone Hall. In July Ar——, that is, Mr. Ferris, was in such distress that I resolved to aid him by obtaining from Miss Gilmar the diamond necklace which had belonged to his father."

"I know," said Gebb, who was listening attentively, "the necklace which Dean gave Laura Kirkstone."

"Yes; it was a family jewel, and Dean gave it to Laura only because she was to be his wife. When she died, it should have been returned to Dean—or, as he was a convict—to his son. Miss Gilmar, however, seized it, and all the rest of Laura's jewels. With the other jewels I had nothing to do, but I was resolved to obtain the necklace for Arthur. Was it not right to do so?"

"Yes," rejoined Gebb, promptly, "the necklace certainly belonged to Mr. Ferris, as his father could not benefit by it. But my wonder is how you got it. From what I have heard of Miss Gilmar, I should have thought the task an impossible one."

"It was difficult to obtain it, but I did so in the end. I told you," said Edith, with some colour, "that I did not know Miss Gilmar was at Grangebury. Well, that was not true; for she wrote to me stating that she was living in Paradise Row under the name of Ligram, and in her letter she asked me about some business. I resolved to visit Grangebury, but as I did not know where it was, I asked Arthur to escort me."

"Did he know of your intention?"

"No; but curiously enough the week I wrote to him he was going down to Grangebury to hear a friend lecture. That was on the twenty-fourth of July; so I came up to town, and went with him on that night."

"To the lecture?"

"Well, not at first. The lecture did not begin until close on nine o'clock, and I wished to see Miss Gilmar; so I sent Arthur in to the Town Hall, and intended to join him when I got the necklace. I then

95

visited Miss Gilmar. She was alone in the house, and admitted me herself. She was much alarmed at seeing me, and still more so when I demanded the necklace."

"I don't wonder at it. Did she refuse to give it up?"

"Yes; although she was wearing it at the time. I told her then that if she did not give it up to me for Arthur, I should search for Dean and tell him where she was. Indeed," added Edith, reflectively, "I am not sure but what I did not say that I knew where Dean was."

"But you did not?" said Gebb, looking at her keenly.

"No, certainly not," she rejoined hastily; "but I said so to frighten Miss Gilmar. She was terrified, and implored me not to take the necklace or tell Dean; but I knew that I was acting rightly, so in the end she gave me the necklace, which I put into my pocket, and left at once."

"About what time?"

"About half-past nine, I think. Miss Gilmar seemed anxious to get me away from the house, and almost pushed me out of the front door, which she locked after me. I then went to the Town Hall; but as Arthur was in one of the front seats, and the lecturer was speaking, I did not wish to create a disturbance by joining him, so I sat down near the door. I had some conversation with the doorkeeper as to where Mr. Ferris was seated; so if you ask him, he'll tell you that I sat near him until the lecture concluded, at half-past ten o'clock. Then Arthur joined me in much alarm, as he thought I had got into trouble. We returned to London, where I gave him the necklace, and told him to pawn it and pay his debts. I slept at the Grosvenor Hotel, near the Victoria Station, and Arthur went back to his rooms in Chelsea. So you see, Mr. Gebb, both he and I are quite innocent."

"It seems so," said the cautious Gebb, not committing himself.

"It is so," insisted Edith, haughtily. "The doorkeeper can tell you that both Mr. Ferris and myself were in the Town Hall before and after ten, and it was about that time Miss Gilmar was murdered."

"Was any one with her when you called?"

"No. I told you she was alone; but there was wine on a small table, and with that, and the way she pushed me out, I was sure she expected some one."

"Did you meet any one in the street going there?"

"Not a soul. I saw no one. Everybody in Grangebury seemed to be at the lecture."

"Did you write and tell Mr. Ferris about my visit to you?"

"Yes, I did; and warned him not to pawn the necklace, as he might be suspected. But it was too late, for he pawned it the day after I gave it to him. But he is innocent, as you see, Mr. Gebb. Surely he will be released."

"When his trial takes place he will," said Gebb. "He would have been let off before if he had told this story to the magistrate."

"Ah!" said Edith, in a low voice, "he held his peace for my sake. Good, brave Arthur! No wonder I love him."

CHAPTER XVIII

WHAT MRS. PRESK FOUND

Gebb continued to question and cross-question Edith until he became thoroughly acquainted with the details of her visit to Miss Gilmar at Grangebury. When in full possession of the facts he permitted her to depart, but took the precaution to ask for her London address in case he should require her further evidence. Edith informed him that since leaving Kirkstone Hall she had been staying with an old schoolfellow in Bloomsbury Square, and was likely to remain there for some time, or at all events until she could find a situation.

"I must work, you know, Mr. Gebb," she confessed frankly. "I am very poor."

"Yet had you accepted Mr. Alder you would——"

"Accept Mr. Alder!" interrupted Edith, colouring. "I would sooner sweep the streets than marry any one but Arthur. Mr. Gebb," she added imploringly, "now that you are convinced of his innocence, do get him out of prison."

"I'll do my best," promised the detective. "He will come up for trial in a week or two, but in the mean time if I place the actual facts of the case before the magistrate who committed him, I have no doubt he will be admitted on bail."

"Anything—anything, dear Mr. Gebb, so long as he is set free!"

The detective proved to be as good as his word, and worked zealously in the interest of Ferris. As the forthcoming trial would probably be a mere matter of form, seeing that the later evidence acquitted him, the magistrate readily accepted bail for a small amount, and, to Edith's astonishment, the person who guaranteed it was Mr. Alder. He came forward in the most friendly way to stand security for his rival, and would not even hear of Edith thanking him when Arthur was released through his generosity.

"I knew he was not guilty," said this benefactor to Edith, "and I told Gebb it was a shame keeping an innocent man in prison."

"How can we ever thank you?" said Edith, tearfully.

"There is no need to thank me, Miss Wedderburn. Of course I should like you to marry me; but as Ferris proves to be the lucky man, I can only make the best of my misfortune."

In her own heart Edith could not understand the kindness of Mr. Alder, for up to the present she had always thought him hard-hearted and selfish. Perhaps the succession to the Kirkstone estates had wrought this change, for previous to the death of his cousin the barrister had been in deep water, as Basson frankly told Gebb.

"It's an ill wind that blows nobody any good," said the Bohemian lawyer, "and the wretch who killed that old woman put a power of money into Alder's pocket. He isn't the man to live on nothing; and has rather expensive tastes; so, if he hadn't come in for that property, he'd have been in Queer Street. It's truth I'm telling you." To which latter remark Gebb quite assented, as Alder had rather the worn look of a man who lived hard, and made the most of his life.

"It's a pity Miss Wedderburn doesn't marry him," he observed. "She might keep him in order. He's a ship that needs an anchor, in my opinion."

"Well, well, Mr. Gebb, Ferris is the better man of the two."

"But not the richer. Mr. Alder has offered two hundred pounds reward for the capture of Miss Gilmar's assassin."

"And you intend to earn it, I suppose?" said Basson, smiling.

"If I can; but at present I see no chance of finding the criminal. Upon my word," cried Gebb, in disgust, "against my better judgment I'm beginning to believe that Dean is guilty after all."

"I don't think so; but if that is your idea, why don't you find Dean and tax him with the crime? An interview with him would put the matter beyond all doubt."

"I don't know where to look for him," said Gebb, grumbling. "I think I shall look up Parge about the matter. If any one knows where Dean is to be found, Parge is the man. Yes, I'll see Parge."

"You may see Parge," said Basson, in a tone of contempt, "but it's doubtful if you'll ever see Dean. He has vanished so completely, that I should not be at all surprised to learn that he is dead. If he was alive and in hiding, surely the police would have found him out before now."

"The police only perform miracles in novels," replied Gebb, dryly, and went off to see Parge.

The fat ex-detective received him almost as wrathfully as he had done on the occasion of the previous visit. Gebb had been so busily employed in searching for Miss Gilmar's assassin, that he had foolishly omitted to pay Mr. Parge the attention which that gentleman considered his due; therefore he was greeted by his chief in anything but a friendly way.

"And I don't want to hear any more excuses," said Parge, scowling; "too much time is lost in telling unnecessary lies. Let me know how much further you have got on with the case."

Glad to escape further blame, the detective related all he had discovered in relation to Ferris and Miss Wedderburn. Parge listened attentively, and was gracious enough to signify his approval of Gebb's conduct.

"You have not done badly," he said, with a nod. "Although your discoveries have been due more to good luck than to your own intelligence. If the girl had not confessed about her visit, and her giving of the necklace to Ferris, you would still be in doubt about his innocence."

"No, I wouldn't," protested Gebb. "Before Miss Wedderburn spoke I was quite sure that Ferris was guiltless. Alder's evidence proved that he was at the lecture, at the time the crime was committed."

"It didn't prove how Ferris became possessed of the necklace, however," snapped Parge. "But I don't see that you are much further on than before. Have you examined that doorkeeper as to Miss Wedderburn's presence in the lecture hall on the night and at the hour of the murder?"

"I have not had time, Simon. To-morrow morning I am going down to see him."

"At Grangebury, I suppose?" said Parge. "Will you find the man there?"

"Yes; the doorkeeper is also the caretaker of the hall."

"Then at the same time you had better call on Mrs. Presk. I suppose the goods of Miss Gilmar have been moved by Alder as her heir?"

"Yes! The body was exhumed and has been identified, and now Alder has taken possession of the estates. Prain is attending to all legal matters concerning the will, and, by Alder's direction, he dismantled the Yellow Boudoir. I don't see what I shall gain by seeing Mrs. Presk."

"You can find out if she has discovered anything touching on the first or second murder!"

"I don't quite understand."

"Bah!" cried Parge, angrily. "Can't you understand that a woman would not be left in possession of a dead woman's goods without satisfying her curiosity in some way? I'll bet you, Absalom, that Mrs. Presk has searched in all Miss Gilmar's boxes, and clothes, and papers, to find out what she can about her. Now, it is just possible that Mrs. Presk may have come across that confession you talk about."

"Do you think it exists?" asked Gebb, with some scepticism.

"Yes, I do; that hint in the anonymous letter written to Basson shows that Miss Gilmar had it in her mind to do justice to the man she wronged."

100

"But you declared that Dean was guilty," said Gebb, recalling his first conversation.

"So I did; it seemed so at the time," rejoined Parge, promptly. "But I have altered my mind; especially since you told me about that letter written by Miss Gilmar to Basson. Either she or Laura Kirkstone killed the man. I don't know which, neither do you; so, for the gratification of our mutual curiosity and the clearance of Dean, you had better find that confession."

"Well, Simon, if that confession is anywhere, it is hidden at Kirkstone Hall."

"It might be," replied Parge, cautiously. "On the other hand, Miss Gilmar might have written it after she fled from the Hall, and have carried it about with her from place to place. If Mrs. Presk has found it, she is just the kind of woman, from your description, to make money over it, by refusing to give it up until she gets her own terms. Call on Mrs. Presk, Absalom, and find out the truth."

"I'll do so," said Gebb, making a mental note of this. "But what about Dean?"

"Well, I believe that Dean is guilty of murdering Miss Gilmar," said Parge, "even if he is innocent of the first crime. He committed the second in order to punish the woman who unjustly condemned him. I am sure he had every cause to wish her ill. She treated him most vindictively."

"It is no use our discussing that matter," said Gebb, tartly. "I believe—on arguments I furnished you with before—that Dean is innocent. You think he is guilty; time and discovery may prove which of us is right. The question now is, where is he to be found?"

"I can't say, Absalom. He escaped from prison in 1893, and we hunted for him high and low, but without success. He vanished as completely as though the earth had swallowed him up. I thought myself he might have gone to Kirkstone Hall to kill Miss Gilmar; and I searched the neighbourhood, but he was nowhere to be found. From that day to this not a word has been heard of him."

"I suppose there is no use hunting for him?"

"It is waste of time, to my mind," retorted Parge, crossly. "You see what Mrs. Presk is doing. Question her; question the servant who—— By the way, what is the servant's name?"

"Matilda Crane; but she knows nothing."

"It's as well to ask her, however," warned Parge. "The people who seem to know least usually know most. Now go away, Absalom, and don't be so long in looking me up again. I'm anxious to get to the bottom of this case."

"You can't be more anxious than I am," replied Gebb, disconsolately.

"At all events, I am more hopeful," rejoined Parge, and dismissed his pupil, who went away with the conviction that the old man was worn out—that he was past work—and that no aid or useful advice could be expected from him. But Gebb still had sufficient reverence for his elder not to hint at these things. Besides, Parge might have turned the tables on him had he been too frank.

The next day he went down to Grangebury, and called at the Town Hall to interview the caretaker. He proved to be a smart ex-soldier, with an observant eye and a good memory, which gifts he made use of on the present occasion for the benefit of Gebb, and also of his own pocket.

"I remember the lady quite well," he said, after some thought. "The young gentleman called himself Mr. Ferris, and told me he was going in, but that a lady, by name Miss Wedderburn, would come afterwards; and he asked me to bring her up to where he was sitting in the front seats. She came in about half-past nine o'clock, but refused to let me take her up to the front, as she did not wish to disturb the lecturer. She sat down near the door, and when the lecture ended the young gentleman joined her, and they went out together."

"Were they in the hall before ten o'clock?" asked Gebb.

"Yes, sir. Before ten and after ten. I saw them both."

This unprejudiced testimony put the matter beyond all doubt So Gebb gave the man a florin, and went away quite convinced that Ferris and Edith were innocent. He next called upon Mrs. Presk, and had an interview with that lady, and with her servant. What the landlady told him may be gathered from a conversation later in the day which Gebb had with Edith.

It was in the afternoon when Miss Wedderburn saw him. She was sitting with Arthur in the drawing-room of Mrs. Barrington at Bloomsbury, and they were anxiously discussing the case of Miss Gilmar's death when Gebb was announced. Neither Edith nor her lover was particularly glad to see the detective, as their associations with him had been anything but pleasant. However, Gebb took black looks and short answers as a portion of the ills incidental to his profession, and conversed with the pair in his most amiable and persuasive fashion.

"I have been down to Grangebury to-day," he said, addressing Edith, "and I saw Mrs. Presk, the landlady of your late cousin. From her I obtained a railway ticket, and it is a piece of evidence of such importance that I have come to you and Mr. Ferris about it."

"A railway ticket!" repeated Edith, looking puzzled. "From what station?"

"The ticket," said Gebb, producing it from his pocket-book, "Is

102

dated the twenty-fourth of July, and is a return portion from London to Norminster!"

"It is not mine, then!" cried Miss Wedderburn. "I did not take a return ticket."

"But you came up on the twenty-fourth of July from Norminster, did you not?"

"Certainly; to see Ellen. But I bought a single ticket, second class."

"Second class," said the detective, looking at the ticket; "this is a third class return. Are you sure it isn't yours?"

"Quite sure" said Edith, decisively. "Why should I deceive you about it?"

"Why, indeed!" said Gebb, ironically, with a hint at her former deception. "Is it yours, Mr. Ferris?"

Arthur shook his head. "No. If I travelled at all it would be third class, I admit. But I did not go to Norminster in the month of July."

"I thought so," said Gebb, with an air of relief. "Then as this ticket belongs to neither of you, some third person must have travelled from Norminster to Grangebury on the twenty-fourth of July. And I believe that person," added Gebb, emphatically, "to be the murderer of Miss Gilmar."

"On what grounds?" cried Edith and Arthur together.

"Because Mrs. Presk found this ticket in the Yellow Boudoir. It must have been dropped there by the assassin."

CHAPTER XIX

THE UNEXPECTED OCCURS

Gebb found it impossible to discover the owner of that third-class railway ticket. He went himself to Norminster to find out, if possible, to whom it had been issued, but all in vain. The station-master had taken another situation in Scotland, the ticket clerk was absent on his annual holidays, and none of the porters could remember any particular person who had gone up to London on that particular day. On the whole, circumstances seemed to be against Gebb in following this clue, and after several vain attempts he gave it up, at all events for the present This he confessed to Parge, who at once reproved him for faint-heartedness, and preached a lengthy sermon on the folly of being discouraged.

"You don't expect roast ducks to fly into your mouth, do you?" said Parge, indignantly. "Of course, it is no easy task to hunt down a criminal. We'd have all the bad 'uns in gaol if such was the case. You've only been a week looking after this ticket business, yet you shy off just because you can't find out about it straight away. You never were a detective, Absalom, and you never will be!"

"But just look here," cried the badgered Absalom. "What can I do? I've been——"

"I know where you've been—to Norminster," growled Parge, "and I know what you've done—nothing. You think I'm past work. I saw that the other day. Well, from nat'ral infirmity, or too much fat, so I am; but in nowise else, Absalom, so don't you believe it. If I was in your shoes, which I ain't, I'd write up to that station-master in Scotland, and ask him if he knows of any partic'ler person as left Norminster on that day. It ain't a big place, and if he's a sharp one he might remember."

"I've written to the station-master," cried Gebb, crossly.

"Oh, have you?" returned Parge, rather disappointed. "Then I'll be bound you don't know what you're going to do about that ticket clerk."

"Yes, I do. I'm going to wait till he comes back, and then question him at once. In about a week I'll know all those two know, though I dare say it won't be much. And look you here, Simon," cried Gebb, warming up, "it's all very well your pitching into me over this case; but is it an easy one? 'Cause if you say it is, it ain't. I never in my born days came across such a corker of a case as this

104

one. Who would have thought that Ferris and the girl would be mixed up in it?—yet they were. And who would have thought them guilty? Everybody! And were they guilty? You know they weren't. Can you find Dean? No, you can't, though you tried yourself when his trail was still fresh. Then how the devil do you expect me to find him after all these years? It's very easy to sit in your chair and pick holes, Simon, but when you come to work the case for yourself, you'll be as up a tree as I am at this blessed moment."

"I don't deny that the case is hard, Absalom."

"Hard!" echoed Gebb, with scorn; "it's the most unnat'ral case as ever was. I've only got one blessed clue after all my hard work, and that's the railway ticket; which, so far as I can see, is about as much good as a clock would be to a baby."

"Why don't you question Mrs. Presk?"

"I have questioned her, and the servant too; and beyond the ticket, she don't know a blessed thing."

"Can't Basson help you, or Mr. Alder, or Mr. Ferris?"

"No, none of the three; they don't know who killed Miss Gilmar, and if it comes to a point, Simon, I don't see why they should know."

"It is queer that the lot of them, including the girl, should have been in Grangebury on the very night of the murder," said Parge, with a musing air.

"It's a coincidence, that's all," retorted Gebb, "and you know very well in our profession there's no end of coincidences, though if you write them in a book people tell you they're impossible. You can't accuse any one of the three of killing the old woman, as they were all in the lecture hall the whole evening. You know all about Ferris, and Miss Wedderburn; well, it couldn't have been them. Mr. Basson was lecturing; it couldn't have been him. Mr. Alder was looking after the money and the house, so as to get plenty of cash in for his friend; so it couldn't have been him. If not them, who is guilty?"

"Well, Dean must be the criminal."

"I don't believe it," replied Gebb, obstinately. "And if he is, he'll not be hanged; for old Nick himself couldn't hunt him out. By the way, Simon, what kind of a man was he to look at—to the naked eye, so to speak?"

"I don't know what he'll be like now," replied Parge, briskly; "but he was uncommonly good-looking in the dock, I can tell you. Just the man to take a woman's fancy: tall, and dark and smiling."

"Any particular mark?" asked Gebb, professionally.

"Well, he wasn't scarred or scratched in any way that I know of," replied Parge, reflectively, "but he had a frown."

"Get along! Every one's got a frown," said Gebb, in a disgusted tone.

"Not of his sort," was Parge's answer. "Since sitting here, Absalom, I've been reading a heap of books I never read before. Amongst others one called 'Redgauntlet,' by a baronet, Sir Walter Scott. Know it?"

"No, I don't. What has it got to do with Dean?"

"There was a fellow in it," said Parge, following his own reflections, "as had a horseshoe mark over his nose when he frowned. Quite queer it was."

"Must have been," said Gebb, derisively. "And has Dean a horseshoe?"

"No. But when he scowls, or frowns, like this"—here Parge made a hideous face—"he's got a queer mark, deep as a well and quite straight, between his eyebrows. I'd know him from among a thousand by it. Seems to cut his forehead in two like. If you see a man with a mark like that when he's in a rage, Absalom, just you nab him, for that's Dean."

"Stuff!" said Gebb, impatiently. "Lots of men wrinkle up into lines when they get out of temper. I've seen foreheads like Clapham Junction for lines."

"Not so deep," answered Parge, shaking his head, "and not straight down between the eyes. Most men frown in lines which run across the forehead when they raise their eyebrows like; but Dean draws everything up to a deep mark as dips just between the eyebrows and on to the nose. It's the queerest mark I ever saw; and whatever disguise he puts on he can't smooth that furrow out. A baby could tell him by it."

"Hum!" said Gebb, who had been thinking. "Now you come to talk of it, Simon, that young Ferris has a mark like that, but not very deep."

"He's young yet, Absalom; but I dare say he takes after his father. Well, all I say is that there's no other way in which you'll spot Dean. He may grow old, and white, and shaky, or he may disguise himself in all kinds of ways, but he can't rub out that brand of Cain as Nature has set on him. I said it before, and I say it again."

"I'll look round for a man of that sort," said Gebb, rising to take his leave, "but I can't say I've much hope of finding him. Dean's been lost for so long that I dare say he's lost for ever. Well, good-bye, Simon. I won't see you for a day or two. There's heaps for me to do."

"Where are you going?" grunted the fat man.

"I'm off to ask Mr. Alder to let me search in Kirkstone Hall for that confession of Miss Gilmar's. Then I'm going down there to look it up."

"That won't do any good towards finding out who killed her," said Parge, shaking his head.

"I don't know so much about that, Simon," replied Gebb, coolly. "I wouldn't be a bit surprised to find as the person who killed Kirkstone was some one quite different from those we suspect."

"It must be either Miss G. or Miss K.," said Parge, "and knowing the truth about them won't help you to spot the assassin. You look for Dean first, Absalom, and leave the confession alone for a while."

"No!" replied Gebb, obstinately. "I'll look for the confession, and fly round afterwards for Dean. You let me negotiate the job in my own way, Simon."

With this determination, of which Parge by no means approved, but was unable to hinder, Gebb went off to make his last venture in solving the mystery. By this time he was in a furious rage at his many failures, and swore under his breath that come what might he would hunt down and punish the unknown assassin of the wretched old woman who had been strangled in Paradise Row. He had three designs in his head, one of which he hoped might serve to attain the much-desired end. Firstly, he intended to search for the confession of Miss Gilmar, in the belief that it might throw some light on the later case. Secondly, he resolved to follow the clue of the railway ticket, and learn who had come up from Norminster on that fatal night to visit Miss Gilmar, since such person—on the evidence of the ticket found in the Yellow Boudoir—was undoubtedly her murderer. Thirdly, he was bent upon making another search round the pawnshops to see if any of the other jewels taken from the body had been turned into money. The appearance of the necklace was accounted for by Edith, as she had received it from the old woman before the assassin had arrived; but the rings, bracelets, and hair ornaments were still missing. Sooner or later, in order to benefit by his crime, the murderer would seek to turn them into cash when he thought the storm had blown over. Then was the time to trace and capture him.

The French have a proverb which runs in English, "that nothing is certain but the unforeseen," and certainly Gebb proved the truth of this when he arrived at Alder's lodgings. As yet the barrister, pending the administration of the estate, had not moved from his rooms in the Temple; but he intended to do so shortly, and already had engaged handsome chambers in Half-moon Street. These, however, he was never destined to occupy, for on the very day Gebb called to see him he met with an accident which seemed likely to result in his death. As one pleasure to be gained from his riches,

Alder had purchased a horse, shortly after coming into his fortune, and every morning went riding in the Row. He was a good rider, but not having indulged in the exercise for some years, by reason of his impecuniosity, he had lost a portion of his skill, with the result that the horse, a fiery animal with tricks of which Alder was ignorant, bolted unexpectedly, and threw his rider against the rails. Alder fell across them with such force that he had injured his spine, and now was lying in his rooms in a crippled condition.

"Do you think he'll get over it?" asked Gebb, when Alder's servant was relating the occurrence.

"No, sir," answered the man, shaking his head. "The doctor says he's bound to die sooner or later. The spine is injured, and my poor master can't feel anything below his waist. It's death in life already, and the end is sure to come."

"Can I see him?" asked the detective, after some thought.

"No, sir; the doctor left word that he was to see no one."

With this Gebb was forced to be content; and as already he had obtained Alder's permission to search the Hall, he went away rather low-spirited. It seemed hard that the man should come to an untimely end, just when he inherited his kingdom. Moreover, he had behaved very well in defending Ferris in the face of all evidence, and releasing him from prison; therefore Gebb thought it just as well to send a line to the artist and Edith, so that they might come forward in their turn to do what they could for the man who had acted so generously towards them both.

"It's hard lines," said Gebb to himself, when he had posted his letter. "I do call it hard. Alder gained a fortune, it is true; but he lost the woman he wished to marry, and now he loses his life. It's a queer world, that gives a man a pleasure only to take it away from him again. I don't understand the workings of Providence nohow."

With this philosophical reflection, Gebb went home to make his plans before going down to Norminster the next day. He had little hope of success, however, and now that Alder was dying, he wondered, if he did capture the murderer, if the reward would be paid to him.

"Of course it will," he said to himself on reflection, "for if Alder dies. Miss Wedderburn becomes mistress of the Hall."

CHAPTER XX

A NEEDLE IN A HAYSTACK

It was a bright and sunny day when Gebb found himself once more at Kirkstone Hall. In the sunshine the building looked grim and desolate. The smokeless chimneys, the closed doors, dusty windows, and grass-grown terraces, gave the place a forlorn and wretched aspect; and the absence of life, the silence broken only by the twittering of the birds, the neglected gardens, created, even to the detective's prosaic mind, an atmosphere of menace and dread. It looked like a place with a history; and Gebb wondered if Miss Wedderburn, on becoming its mistress, would care to inhabit it again.

"When she marries Ferris and begins a new life, I dare say she will seek some more cheerful abode," he thought, as he stood on the terrace, and looked on the silent house. "It would be foolish for a young couple to dwell with the ghosts of the past. I am not imaginative myself, but I should not care to live here; no, not if the house was given to me rent free. If I were Miss Wedderburn I'd pull it down and build a new place without a past or a ghost."

While Gebb soliloquized thus, he heard a hoarse voice in the distance, and saw Martin, spade on shoulder, passing across the lawn singing one of his gruesome songs. Evidently he had caught sight of the detective on the terrace, for not until he came towards him did he begin to sing. Then he danced grotesquely over the green turf, croaking his wild ditty, and looking a strange figure in the strong sunshine; yet not unsuited to the lonely place, with its grim associations:—

> "When moon shines clear my shadow and I
> Dance in the silver light;
> When moon lies hid in a cloudy sky
> My shadow with her takes flight.
> And I remain, in the falling rain,
> Calling upon my shadow in vain:
> 'Oh, shadow dear, I wait you here,
> Alone in the lonely night.'"

When he came close to Gebb he stopped his song and dance suddenly, and looked inquiringly at the detective with his head on

109

one side. "What do you want?" he croaked. "There is nothing here but death and misery."

"I've come to look at the house, Martin. Can you show me over it?"

"No, no," said the gardener, shaking his head. "I don't walk through the valley of dry bones. If you sit in the Yellow Room you hear the dead tell secrets."

"What kind of secrets?" asked Gebb, humouring him.

"How the sister killed the brother, and how she who killed them both laughed and laughed.

> 'But she died at last in deep despair
> When Satan caught her in his snare.'"

Gebb looked fixedly at the man. He had been in the house at the time of the Kirkstone murder, so it might be that his poor wits retained a memory of the tragedy. Was it possible that light could be thrown on its darkness by this madman? The detective asked himself that question once or twice as he listened to the poor creature rambling on, how Laura had killed her brother at the instigation of Miss Gilmar.

"And is Mr. Dean innocent?" he asked suddenly.

"God and His saints know that he had no hand in it!" cried Martin, with a remarkably sane look on his face. "A woman ruined one, a woman slew the other; and the poor soul lies in chains—in chains." And he fell to weeping, as though his heart would break with sorrow and pain.

"I wonder if this is the truth," thought Gebb. "Perhaps, after all, Laura did murder her brother, and Miss Gilmar to save her denounced Dean. But there is no sense to be got out of this lunatic; his evidence would not stand in a court of law. The only thing is to search for that confession, so the sooner I set to work the better.—Martin," he said, aloud, "can you show me over the house?"

"Not I! Not I! Ask old Jane. Come, and I'll take you to old Jane;" and shouldering his spade again, Martin walked off round the comer of the terrace, singing:—

> "God it far away, alas!
> The Devil is beside us;
> And as we wander thro' the world,
> He is the one to guide us.
>
> "He gives with grin, the wage of sin;
> And when the fiend hath paid us,

110

We stand outside the gate of Hell,
With Christ alone to aid us."

Old Jane proved to be a grim and elderly female in a rusty black dress and a still rustier bonnet She came out of a side door, and wiping her hands on a coarse apron, curtsied to Gebb, while Martin, introducing the pair with a regal wave of the hand, danced off round the corner.

"What may you be pleased to want?" asked old Jane, when the scarecrow gardener had disappeared.

"I have received permission from Mr. Alder to look over the house," replied the detective, "and I wish you to show it to me."

"There ain't much to see, sir," croaked the ancient dame, "it's all dust and darkness. I doubt if my old legs would carry me over it."

"Oh, well, I can go by myself, Jane," said Gebb, cheerfully.

"Mrs. Grix, if you please!" snapped Jane, indignantly. "I only allows Miss Edith to call me by my first name. Poor pretty dear, and she's gone away for ever."

"I wouldn't be too sure of that," rejoined Gebb, dryly. "Mr. Alder has met with an accident and may die; in which case Miss Wedderburn will return here as mistress."

"Mr. Alder's ill, is he?" said Jane, in no very regretful tone, "and may die. Ah, well," with a lachrymose whine, "all flesh is grass, that it is; and if Miss Edith does come back I hope she'll shut up the Yeller Room."

"For what reason, Mrs. Grix?"

"'Cause it's haunted by spirits," replied Mrs. Grix, with a mysterious look. "I've heard the two of 'em quarrelling there."

"Which two? What two?" asked Gebb, who began to think that the old lady had been at the bottle.

"Miss Gilmar and the master; they 'aunts the Yeller Room and fights. I knows it; 'cause I sleeps here all alone, save for Martin as lives in the back part; an' I hears voices, that I do."

"I wonder you are not more afraid of that madman than of ghosts."

Mrs. Grix smiled in a cunning and significant manner. "Oh, I ain't afraid of Martin, sir; no one as knows him fears him."

"And why?" asked Gebb, sharply.

This question Mrs. Grix did not choose to hear; but mumbling and shaking her old head, hobbled along the passages in the direction of the Yellow Room. She ushered Gebb into this with a chuckle, and threw open the shutters to let the sunlight shine on the faded and time-worn decorations of the room.

"I s'pose you'll want to see this first," said Mrs. Grix; "most

111

folks likes to see a room as a murder's been done in. There's a stain of blood over in that corner—master's blood, which Miss Gilmar would never let be wiped out I dessay master comes and looks at it, and wishes he had his body again. He was an awful bad one—and mean!" Mrs. Grix lifted up a pair of dirty and trembling hands. "They was both of 'em skinflints," said she, with a nod.

"Whom are you speaking of, Mrs. Grix?"

"Of Miss Gilmar and Mr. Kirkstone, sir."

"Did you know them?"

"Did I know them?" echoed the hag, with scorn. "Of course I knowed them; and a bad lot the pair of 'em was. They give Miss Laurer a fine time, I can tell you. I wonder she didn't go off with Mr. Dean, I do."

"Were you here when the murder took place?" asked Gebb.

"Lor' bless yer 'eart, I sawr the 'ole of it," croaked Mrs. Grix. "Master was a-lying over there with a knife in his 'eart, and Miss Gilmar, she was 'ollering for the police."

"Did Dean kill Kirkstone?"

"Ah, that's telling!" said Mrs. Grix, cunningly. "Don't you ask no questions, young man, and you won't be told no lies."

"You must tell me!" cried Gebb, seizing her by the wrist "I am from Scotland Yard—a detective." And he shook the beldame furiously.

Mrs. Grix raised a feeble wail of horror.

"Lor', you're perlice, are you?" she whimpered. "Jist let me go; I know nothin'."

"Did Laura Kirkstone kill her brother?"

"I dunno; I swear I dunno."

"Was Miss Gilmar the criminal?"

Mrs. Grix leered. "She never told me she was, sir, but she didn't carry the Yeller Room about with her for nothing."

"What do you mean?" said Gebb, releasing her.

Mrs. Grix rubbed her wrist, which had been somewhat bruised by his clasp, and leered again. "Miss Gilmar wrote it all down," she said.

"A confession?" cried the detective.

"I dunno what you call it, sir; but I know she wrote it down, 'cause she said to me, 'It'll be all right when I'm dead.' Well, she are dead," said Mrs. Grix, "and it ain't all right, unless she left the writin' behind her."

"Where is that confession?"

"I dunno. I wish I did. There's money in it. I've hunted all over the 'ouse, and I can't come across it nohow."

"Well, Mrs. Grix, what is your opinion? Was it Dean, or Miss Gilmar, or Miss Laura who killed the man?"

"You look about for the paper, lovey," said Mrs. Grix, coaxingly, "and it'll tell ye all."

"You tell me."

"But I don't know for certain."

"Never mind. What is your opinion?"

"Will ye give me money for it?"

"That depends upon your information."

"Then I shan't tell ye," cried Mrs. Grix, backing towards the door. "You can look for what she wrote. I shan't 'elp you. Keep me fro' the work-'ouse, and maybe I'll tell ye summat to make you wink; but not now, not now. Old Jane Grix ain't no fool, lovey. No, no!"

Gebb made a step forward to detain her, but Mrs. Grix hobbled through the door and vanished in the darkness as mysteriously as any of the ghosts she had been talking about. At all events, when the detective slipped out of the Yellow Room and into the twilight of the passage, his eyes were somewhat dazzled by the sunlight and glare of colour within, and he saw nothing for the moment, Mrs. Grix was quicker on her old feet than he supposed, and in some way hobbled out of sight into one of the numerous passages, so that when Gebb's eyes became accustomed to the gloom he did not know into which one she had gone. Also he heard rapidly retreating footsteps—not the heavy hobble of the old woman, but rather the light, dancing step of Martin. And as to confirm this impression he heard the hoarse voice of the gardener singing one of his wild songs:—

"Light shall come, but not from above,
Joy shall come, but not from love,
The glow of hell, the lust of hate,
Impatiently for these I wait."

"Ha!" said Gebb to himself, as he hurried down the passage. "Martin has been listening. I wonder why? I don't believe he is mad, after all, for neither that old woman nor Miss Wedderburn is afraid of him. He must be feigning madness for some reason. Ha!" cried the detective with a sudden start, "can Martin be the murderer of—"

Before he could finish the sentence he heard a series of piercing shrieks from Mrs. Grix, and a hoarse growling from Martin. These noises sounded far in the distance, and Gebb ran down the passage, through the sitting-room into which he had been shown by Miss Wedderburn on the occasion of his first visit, and on to the terrace. Here he saw Mrs. Grix running from Martin, who was rushing after her with a furious face. Gebb stared, not at the terrified old woman,

113

who was hurrying towards him with wonderful activity for one of her years, but at Martin's face. It wore a savage scowl, and there between the eyes was the deep mark spoken of by Parge.

"Dean!" cried Gebb, thunderstruck. "You are Dean!"

"Yes! yes!" screeched Mrs. Grix, getting behind Gebb, "he's Dean sure enough. He was going to kill me 'cause I wanted to tell ye."

Martin—or rather Dean—stopped when he heard his name, then turned, and leaping over the terrace ran like a hare down the avenue.

CHAPTER XXI

FOUND AT LAST

On seeing the pseudonymous gardener speeding down the avenue, Gebb lost no time, but, leaving Mrs. Grix to her rage and lamentation, vaulted over the terrace in his turn, and raced at top speed after the fugitive. The detective was lean and young, and an excellent runner, whereas Dean, alias Martin, was old and scant of breath; so the only thing which equalized the contest was the despair which winged the feet of the wretched quarry. If Dean were caught by the bloodhound of the law, he would be shortly relegated to the prison whence he had escaped; so he flew wildly over the ground, running he knew not whither to escape the fate which awaited him. And Gebb, who personified Nemesis, followed hot-footed in his track.

The road to Norminster ran straight through the fields like a white ribbon laid upon green velvet, and the town itself was distant a mile from Kirkstone Hall. Down this, amid a cloud of white dust, Gebb saw Dean running some way ahead, and setting his elbows to his sides he followed steadily and surely, reserving his wind for the termination of the race, the result of which could only be the capture of the ragged figure now flying for dear life. Carters, and pedestrians, and labourers in the fields stared in amazement at the chase, and some, with that love of sport inherent in every breast, joined Gebb in his man-hunt. After Dean had covered a quarter of a mile he began to fail, and to zigzag in his course, bounding wildly from one side to the other, and wasting his strength in useless ways. Gebb with his shouting train drew steadily nearer, and the miserable, hunted wretch could hear their cries, and the beating of their feet on the hard white road. Still he endeavoured to shake off his pursuers and escape, for by a powerful effort he managed to run another quarter of a mile. Then age and fear and exhaustion told on his failing limbs, and with a wild cry Dean flung up his hands despairingly and fell amid puffs of dust. When Gebb arrived he was lying senseless in the middle of the highroad.

"So!" said the detective to himself, as he knelt beside the ragged creature. "I've found you at last, Mr. Dean. You know the truth of all these matters, at any rate; and in some way or another I'll force you into confessing it."

But at the present moment it seemed as though Dean would

never speak again in this world, for he lay as still as any corpse, his white head and whiter face resting on Gebb's knee. The frowning mark between the eyes, by which the detective had known him, was smoothed away, and there was no expression on the blank countenance, no movement in the slack limbs. Gebb, however, knew that this apparent death was only a temporary faintness, and whipping out his brandy-flask, forced some drops of the fiery liquid between the white lips of his prisoner. While engaged in this kindly office, the labourers who had joined in the pursuit came up with much amazement expressed on their honest, sunburnt faces.

"What's the matter with Mad Martin, mister?" asked one, looking at the unconscious Dean.

"He's madder than usual, that's all," said Gebb, "and has nearly killed Mrs. Grix at the Hall yonder. I must take him to Norminster and get a doctor to look after him: he'll die here."

The detective made this artful speech with the intention of enlisting the sympathy of the bystanders, both for himself and Martin, alias Dean, as popular feeling generally inclines towards defiance of law and order. Moreover, a detective is not an admired character with the common people, and Gebb had no desire to render his task of capturing Dean more difficult than was necessary by stating his vocation; so for diplomatic reasons he spoke as above. The result justified his precaution, for the labourers were most anxious that the mad gardener—as they knew him to be—should be taken at once to Norminster and placed in charge of a medical man. A cart was coming along the road, and into this Dean was hoisted by friendly hands. Gebb having taken his seat beside him, the vehicle rolled slowly towards Norminster, while the labourers returned to their work, quite vivacious after the exciting episode which had broken the monotony of the day. Gebb, knowing what was at stake, felt thankful to get rid of them so easily.

As it was but half a mile to Norminster from the spot where Dean had fallen, the cart soon arrived there. The man himself had revived, thanks to Gebb's brandy, and sat staring straight before him in a kind of sullen stupor. He made one effort to escape when he was set down at the door of the gaol; but Gebb, with the assistance of a near policeman, soon overpowered him, and carried him within, while the carter drove off, wondering, in his slow-thinking mind, that a man brought to see a doctor should be taken to the county gaol for care. However, he had received five shillings from Gebb, so did not trouble his head about the matter, and spent most of it at the next public-house, where he narrated the episode with such additions as his drunken humour suggested.

To the governor of the gaol Gebb explained that Dean was an

escaped prisoner, for whom the police had long been looking, and mentioned his own name and occupation. The result of this was that Dean was confined in a cell with a warder to watch him lest he should in his despair attempt suicide. Then Gebb repaired to an hotel and wrote to the governor of the gaol whence Dean had escaped, asking him to come down himself or send some responsible person in order to identify the prisoner. The detective also sent an urgent wire to Ferris, requesting him to visit Norminster at once on business connected with Martin; for he shrewdly suspected that the artist knew of the man's identity with Dean, and that the mention of the name would bring both Arthur and Edith immediately to Kirkstone Hall. It was shortly after midday when Gebb sent this telegram, so he quite expected that if matters stood as he imagined Ferris would come down, and not alone; for if Ferris knew that Martin was his father, Edith also must be in the secret, and, no doubt, she would accompany him. Then Gebb, who was really angry with the young couple for their many concealments, determined to have a thorough explanation of their strange behaviour. These important matters having been attended to, Gebb returned to the gaol and saw Dean; but the interview proved to be anything but a success. Whether the man was mad or not Gebb could not decide without evidence; but certainly his present sullen silence formed a strange contrast to his former excitement. He neither talked recklessly nor sang his wild songs. His limbs were at rest, and his eyes looked dull, although formerly they had been bright and glittering. With vacant gaze and a sullen expression, he sat huddled up in a corner of his cell and absolutely refused to speak or even notice his questioner. The man was thoroughly exhausted and worn out; but Gebb left the cell with the firm conviction that Dean was perfectly sane, and that his madness had been feigned to more effectually baffle dangerous inquiries. But, like the fox in the fable, for all his tricks the man had been caught at last, and Gebb wondered if, after all, he had murdered Miss Gilmar.

"Did that return third-class ticket dropped in the room at Paradise Row belong to Dean?" the detective asked himself. "I should not be surprised if it did. As Miss Wedderburn denies that it is hers, Dean, under the name of Martin, is the only person who could have used it. In that case he must have remained in London all night; for, as the crime was committed at ten o'clock, he could not have caught a return train so late to Norminster. Now, Mrs. Grix lives in the Hall, so she is the most likely person to let me know if Dean was absent on the twenty-fourth of July. I'll see her at once and get to know all I can, pending the arrival of Ferris and Miss

117

Wedderburn. They may deny Dean's complicity in the crime, so I must be prepared to baffle them."

Having made up his mind to question Mrs. Grix, the detective, making a hurried meal, walked out to Kirkstone Hall, and arrived to find the old woman solacing herself with gin-and-water after the fatigues of the morning. She was excessively nervous when Gebb reappeared, as she was conscious she had said too much in her rage with Martin, and now guessed that she was about to be thoroughly examined touching all she knew concerning him. Mrs. Grix, to save her own skin, was quite prepared to equivocate, and Gebb guessed as much, for he went to work with her in a severe official way which frightened her considerably.

"Now, Mrs. Grix," said he, when they were comfortably established in the kitchen, "I've come to ask you a few questions."

"I don't know nothin', I don't," protested Mrs. Grix, beginning her tactics.

"You know a great deal," replied Gebb, sharply. "And if you don't answer me truthfully, I'll arrest you on suspicion and put you in gaol 'longside of Dean; so now you know."

"Lawk-a-mussy!" squealed Mrs. Grix, "have you put him in prison?"

"Yes, I have; so you tell me the truth, or I'll put you in also!"

"I'll speak out, sir," cried the old wretch, much terrified. "I don't want to go to prison. I've done nothing."

"You have spied and listened and searched," retorted Gebb, "all for the sake of gaining possession of other people's secrets and extracting blackmail when possible. Now you answer my questions, or it will be the worse for you."

"I'm willing, sir," said Mrs. Grix, meekly; "but I don't know as much as you think. I only suspects like."

"Can you tell me who killed Kirkstone?" asked the detective.

"That's one thing I don't know for certain," replied the dame; "but if you arsk me, sir, I bel've as Miss Gilmar did."

"On what grounds do you suspect her?"

"Becose she wrote out summat telling the truth and hid it; and she wouldn't have done that, unless she were guilty. Then she were in love with Mr. Dean, and Mr. Kirkstone wanted him to marry Miss Laura; so I thinks as Miss Ellen got 'em both out of the way. She was a clever one, was Miss Ellen."

"Do you know where the confession is?"

"No, I don't. Martin was always hunting for it to clear himself, but if he found it he didn't tell me."

"And Martin is Dean?"

"Yes, he is. It ain't no good tellin' lies, lovey! He is Dean!"

118

"I thought there was a gardener here at the time of the murder called Martin?"

"There was," replied Mrs. Grix, coolly. "And he was queer, too, I tell you; but not as queer as this Martin. I knowed he was Dean as soon as I clapped eyes on him, though he was sorely altered from the 'andsome man he was."

"Then he impersonated Martin to save himself from the police?"

"He did; he's no more mad than I am; but he thought it was safer to pretend being crazy. His songs was awful," said Mrs. Grix, shuddering.

"Did Miss Wedderburn know the truth?"

"Of course, sir! And when she knowed as I knowed, she tole me to 'old my tongue, and paid me for doing it; but she didn't give much, lovey!"

"Did Mr. Ferris know?"

"Seeing as Mr. Dean's his own born father—which I knowed fro' listening to 'm talking—he did."

"Did Dean kill Miss Gilmar?"

Mrs. Grix did not reply to this question with her former glibness. "I don't rightly know of that," she said slowly. "If he did, it wasn't here, for Miss Ellen was in London this long time."

"Was Dean ever in London while he stayed here under the name of Martin?"

"Yes, he was. And just about the time of the murder. It was in July Miss Ellen died, wasn't it?"

"It was," replied Gebb, eagerly, "on the twenty-fourth of July."

"Ah, well, I shouldn't be surprised if Dean did kill her. He was always talking of punishing her," continued Mrs. Grix, with relish; "but I didn't think he'd go so far as murder."

"What makes you think that he did?" asked Gebb.

"Why," said Mrs. Grix, nodding, "he was up in London in July, and he stayed there all night."

"On the twenty-fourth?"

"I can't be sure, sir, but it was at the end of the month. And when he came back he was queerer than ever. Oh, I dessay he went up to kill Miss Ellen," said Mrs. Grix, with conviction. "I can't swear to it, but I'm sure he did; and serve her right, too."

CHAPTER XXII

A SECRET HOARD

On concluding the examination of Mrs. Grix—which lasted some time, owing to the inherent objection of that lady to speak the truth—Gebb spent the afternoon in searching the house for Miss Gilmar's confession. By this time he had quite adopted the opinion of Mrs. Grix regarding the guilt of the former housekeeper, and, on the same authority, he was certain that she had written out and hidden away an account of her crime. The question was, where was it concealed? For the house was so large and rambling, and dusty and dusky, that Gebb almost despaired of finding the paper. At first he thought it might be hidden in the Yellow Room. In that fatal apartment the crime had been committed, and, to keep her perpetually in mind of Dean's threat against her life, the wretched woman had lived during her concealment in a precisely similar apartment, decorated and furnished in the same manner; so, seeing that she had attached such importance to it, the probability was that she had hidden the paper within its precincts. But a strict examination of floor, walls, carpet, hangings, and furniture proved that the confession was not there. Gebb was disgusted at this result and turned his attention to the rest of the house.

In the few hours he had to himself he examined nearly every room in the place, not forgetting the sleeping apartments of Dean and Mrs. Grix, which were situated in the back part of the house. He made several discoveries of more or less importance, but the object of his search he failed to find. Towards five o'clock he gave up hunting for this needle in a haystack—for the search was quite as difficult and impossible—and repaired hot and dusty to Mrs. Grix. From the old woman he obtained water to wash in, and a brush for his clothes, and afterwards she supplied him with a cold supper and beer. Just as Gebb finished this, feeling very refreshed, he heard the sound of voices, and stepped on to the terrace to find that Ferris and Edith had arrived. They both looked pale and nervous, and the grim way in which the detective eyed them inspired neither with confidence.

"We are here, you see," said Ferris, as Edith seemed unwilling to speak, "but neither Miss Wedderburn nor myself can guess the reason of your very peremptory telegram."

"I think you know the reason very well," said Gebb, grimly,

120

"else you would not be here. However, there is no need to talk secrets in the open, so if you will come with me to the Yellow Boudoir, we can speak more at our ease—and perhaps more openly," finished the detective, with a dry cough.

Edith looked at her lover in a quick, terrified manner, but judged it wiser to make no remark, and the two meekly followed Gebb into the Yellow Room. Here they sat down side by side on the primrose-hued couch, while Gebb, after glancing outside to see that Mrs. Grix was not listening, closed and locked the door. Then he drew a chair in front of the couch, and surveyed the pair in no very friendly manner.

"Well, Miss Wedderburn and Mr. Ferris," he said, with much displeasure, "It seems I have to find out things for myself."

"What things?" asked Edith, flushing; for, not knowing the extent of Gebb's knowledge, neither she nor Ferris was prepared to speak freely.

"Things which you know. Miss Wedderburn, and about which you could have informed me. If I had known then what I know now," added Gebb, with emphasis, "I might have had less trouble and more result in this murder case."

"I don't understand you," faltered Ferris, doubtfully.

"You may understand me better when I tell you that your father is in prison again."

"My father? Dean?"

"Yes, Dean or Martin—whichever you like to call him."

"Do you mean to say that Mad Martin, the gardener, is really Mr. Dean?" said Edith, making a final attempt to baffle Gebb.

"Yes, Miss Wedderburn, I do; and why should you or Mr. Ferris there pretend ignorance of what you know to be true? I recognized Dean myself from a description given by Parge. No one can mistake that mark between the eyes when he frowns—which mark, I see, Mr. Ferris has at this moment. And to make sure that Martin is Dean, I have the evidence of Mrs. Grix."

"Mrs. Grix! Has she told you——"

"She has told me everything," interrupted Gebb; "and Dean tried to punish her for talking. Then he ran away, and I chased him into Norminster, where he now lies in gaol."

"But he is mad!" said Ferris, eagerly.

"Who is mad?" demanded Gebb, turning on him. "Your father, or Martin the gardener?"

Ferris made a despairing gesture. "Since you know so much," he said in low tones, "I admit that the two are one and the same. Martin is really my father, Marmaduke Dean, who has been concealed here; but he is insane."

121

"He is nothing of the sort, Mr. Ferris. His insanity was feigned for the better baffling of the police. Neither you nor Miss Wedderburn can deceive me any longer. You have kept silence, you have told untruths, and altogether have given me endless trouble, but now I must insist upon your speaking out, both of you. This time I know so much that you cannot deceive me; and I'll force you to speak."

"Suppose we refuse?" cried Edith, indignant at this rough speech.

"If you do I'll arrest you both as accessories after the fact to the murder of Miss Gilmar. Ah, you look afraid! But I know—I know. Dean murdered that woman, and you are both aware of it."

"My father is innocent!" cried Arthur, with a groan.

"If he is, what was he doing at Grangebury on the evening of the murder? Why did he stay in London all night? What was his return ticket to Norminster doing in Miss Gilmar's room at Paradise Row? The man is guilty, I tell you. Defend him if you can. Tell the truth if you dare, and for once both of you act honourably and straightforwardly."

The detective spoke with much vehemence, and rising from his seat walked rapidly up and down the room. Much as Edith resented his language, yet she was conscious that in a great measure it was deserved. For this reason she restrained her passion and spoke frankly and to the purpose.

"Mr. Gebb," she said, and the detective paused to listen, "I do not deny that much you say is true. Neither myself nor Mr. Ferris have spoken so openly as we might have done. But you must not forget that we had much that was dangerous to ourselves to conceal. If we had told you about the necklace, you might have suspected us of the crime, and it was dread of such danger which kept us silent."

"I know that you are both innocent," said Gebb, coldly. "But about Dean?"

"We did not speak of Dean—of my father—for the same reason," struck in Arthur, earnestly. "He was imprisoned for a crime which he did not commit, and you would not have had me—his own son—betray him."

"Perhaps not; it is a hard thing to ask," responded the detective. "But now that I know so much, perhaps you will tell me more, and inform me how it was that your father came here, and when it was that you first recognized him."

"Certainly," replied Arthur, with a glance at Edith for permission to speak. "I heard almost immediately about my father's escape from prison, and, knowing his hatred for Miss Gilmar, I came to Kirkstone Hall, thinking he might go there to revenge himself. However, although he had not come, Miss Gilmar, with a guilty conscience, no doubt, took fright, and went to hide herself in London. On my first visit I met Miss Wedderburn, and afterwards I frequently came to see her. One day while I was here, an old man arrived and asked to see Miss Gilmar. I saw him, and so did Miss Wedderburn; and when he heard my name, and had examined me carefully, he saluted me as his son. At first I could scarcely believe that he was my father, as I had not seen him for close on twenty years, and was too young to retain much recollection of him. But he soon proved to me that he was Marmaduke Dean, and told us how he had escaped."

"Did he come to the Hall to kill Miss Gilmar?" asked Gebb, anxiously.

"No!" said Ferris, with emphasis. "That threat was uttered only in his mad passion. All he wanted from her was proof of his innocence."

"And I wrote to her about it," said Edith, taking up the tale; "but she was afraid of Mr. Dean, and swore that he killed Mr. Kirkstone."

"Though I am certain," interposed Arthur, "that she killed him herself, and accused my father because she was jealous of his love for Laura."

"That may be," said Gebb, nodding; "but proceed with your story."

"Let me tell the rest," cried Miss Wedderburn. "Mr. Dean was so broken down and ill with the life he had led in prison, that I suggested he should stay here and let me look after him. The police had been to the Hall, and not having found him there, had left. I did not think they would come again, so I believed that Mr. Dean would be quite safe. So he stayed for a day or so, until Mrs. Grix recognized him, but I bribed her with money to silence. She suggested that for safety Mr. Dean should pretend to be Martin—a gardener not quite right in his head, who had left the Hall after the tragedy. It was twenty years since he had gone, and Mr. Dean was much altered from his former self; so in the end he adopted the name of Martin, and pretended to be mad. So now you know, Mr. Gebb, when you saw me first, the reason why I was not afraid of his madness. You thought it real; I knew it to be feigned."

"Did every one round here think he was really Martin come back?"

"Yes. But he kept within the Hall grounds, and saw few people. These left him alone because of his madness. So there is the truth, Mr. Gebb."

"Not all the truth," said Gebb, significantly. "You have not told me how he killed Miss Gilmar."

"He did not kill her!" cried Ferris, furiously.

"He did!" insisted Gebb. "He was in Grangebury on the twenty-fourth of July."

"Impossible!" said Edith, much alarmed. "I did not know that. But even if he was," she went on, "it does not prove that he killed the woman."

"It's pretty good as circumstantial evidence," said Gebb, coolly; "but I have another and stronger proof. Look here," and out of his pocket the detective took a canvas bag, which, when opened, displayed bracelets rings, and diamond stars.

"Miss Gilmar's jewels!" cried Edith, recognizing them at once.

"Yes," said Gebb, "Miss Gilmar's jewels, which I found concealed in Dean's bedroom."

CHAPTER XXIII

THE CONVICT'S DEFENCE

Shaking in the body and white in the face, Ferris looked upon the jewellery, which seemed positive evidence of his father's guilt, then flung himself back on the couch with a groan, his hand over his eyes to shut out the terrible sight—for terrible it was to him, the son of Marmaduke Dean. Edith also gazed fearfully upon the heap of gold and glittering stones, not doubting the truth of Gebb's story.

"Yes!" said the detective, raking the jewels together and replacing them in the bag. "In looking for Miss Gilmar's confession I found these in the room of Dean. They were hidden on the top of a tall press in a dark corner, and I felt, rather than saw them. The case against your father is clear enough, Mr. Ferris, although I was doubtful of it at first. Mrs. Grix can prove that he spent the night of the twenty-fourth of July away from the Hall. The ticket I found in Miss Gilmar's room shows that he must have been there, since no one but he could have possessed, in this especial instance, a ticket from Norminster to London. I'll have the evidence of the station-master and the ticket-clerk to prove his purchase of it shortly, and finally the possession of this jewellery places the matter beyond all doubt."

"There must be some mistake," said Edith, when she found her tongue, "for, although the evidence is against Mr. Dean, I can't believe him guilty. He is an old, broken-down man, timid and cowed. To plan and carry out so ingenious and remorseless a crime would need more spirit and determination than he is possessed of. Besides," she added, very reasonably, "If, as we all think, Mr. Dean is guiltless of Kirkstone's death, why should he kill Miss Gilmar?"

"That is rather an argument against than in favour of him," said Gebb, quietly. "If she condemned him unjustly, and bore false witness against him, as I truly believe she did, that very fact would make him all the more anxious to punish her for such perjury. What do you think, Mr. Ferris?"

"What can I think?" groaned the young man. "The evidence seems to prove my father's guilt. Still, on the face of it, I agree with Miss Wedderburn; he cannot be guilty. Innocent men have been hanged on evidence as conclusive; yet afterwards the truth has come to light. A judge and jury found him guilty of Kirkstone's murder, which we are now certain he did not commit, so it is possible that, despite the evidence to the contrary, he may be innocent of this second crime. Mr. Gebb!" added Ferris, entreatingly, "you know the whole of this matter, and are more experienced in such cases than Miss Wedderburn and myself. Tell us truly—Do you believe in my father's guilt?"

The detective hesitated, and, looking from one to the other, rubbed his chin in a perplexed manner. "I shall answer you honestly, Mr. Ferris," said he, after a pause. "I am not certain of your father's guilt. I said that the possession of this jewellery placed the matter beyond doubt; but against that I must place the fact—established by strong circumstantial evidence—that Miss Gilmar received her assassin as a friend. She was afraid of Dean, and even after the lapse of twenty years she must have recognized him. In place of giving him wine and cigarettes, her impulse would have been to cry out for help. Moreover, without knowing all about her visitor—presuming he was disguised—she would not have let him into her house. On the whole I am doubtful. The fact of the jewellery being found in his room proves his guilt; the fact that Miss Gilmar conversed with him as a friend shows his innocence. Who can decide the matter?"

"I know!" said Edith, suddenly—"Mr. Dean himself. You say that he is in Norminster gaol, Mr. Gebb. Well, that is only a mile from here, so let us all three go there and question Mr. Dean. With this evidence for and against him, he must either declare his innocence or admit his guilt."

"It is the most straightforward course," said Gebb, with a nod. "What do you say, Mr. Ferris?"

"I am content to abide by my father's word," replied Arthur, rising. "Anything is better than this uncertainty. Let us go to Norminster gaol."

"It's rather late," said Gebb, glancing at his watch. "However, I dare say we shall have no difficulty in seeing the prisoner. Come along!"

In the then tumble-down, deserted condition of Kirkstone Hall there was no vehicle obtainable, but the evening was pleasant and Norminster no great distance away, so the three walked briskly along the road in the cool, grey twilight. Conversing about the case made the way seem short, and they soon arrived in the little town and halted before the gates of the gaol. A word from Gebb procured them instant admittance, and they were shown into the presence of the Governor, a retired major, with a bluff manner and a twinkling eye, which was not unobservant of Edith's good looks.

"Well, sir," said Gebb, almost immediately, "and how is your prisoner?"

126

"Clothed and in his right mind!" replied the Governor. "He has given over his sulking and feigned madness, and evidently seems resolved to make the best of things. Indeed, I shouldn't be surprised, Mr. Gebb, if he intended to make you his father-confessor, for he has asked several times after you."

"Good!" said Gebb, rubbing his hands. "This looks like business; he has thrown up the sponge."

"Will you see him now?" asked the Governor, with a side glance at Edith.

"At once, if you please; and I wish this lady and gentleman to be admitted with me."

"Well, it is hardly regular to admit strangers at this hour, Mr. Gebb," said the Major. "Still, as you captured the man, and it is as well for you to hear his confession, if he wishes to make it, I am content to accede to your request. Have you any interest in the matter?" he asked, looking at Edith inquisitively.

"Yes, The man was hidden in my place under the name of Martin," she replied with a blush, not deeming it wise to further enlighten the Governor.

"Indeed. You are Miss Wedderburn, of the Hall? I thought so. Well, go along, all of you, but don't remain more than half an hour with the prisoner. I have to lock up for the night shortly; and I may be tempted to keep so fair a lady in my castle, you know."

Laughing at his own mild joke, the Governor gave his visitors over to the guidance of a warder; and they were soon ushered into a cell, where they found Dean sitting on his bed, chatting cheerfully with the man who watched him. He sprang up to receive them, and after the warder had exchanged a few words with the watcher, they both withdrew, leaving the lamp in the cell. Gebb was much gratified by this mark of the Governor's trust, and spoke to Dean with great complacency.

"I see you have come to your senses, Mr. Dean," he said civilly enough, but with point. "It is about time, I think."

"As you say, about time," replied Dean, who had been greeting Edith and his son. "I have given over fighting against the injustice of the world. I was condemned, an innocent man, some twenty years ago, and I escaped from my prison in the vain hope of getting Ellen Gilmar to prove my innocence; but she is dead, and I am again in the hands of—I won't say justice, but injustice."

"But why did you kill Miss Gilmar?" asked Gebb; for Ferris and Edith sat by quietly, letting him conduct the conversation, as the most capable person.

"I did not kill Miss Gilmar," replied Dean, firmly and sadly.

127

"God knows who sent that wicked woman to her last account, but it was not I."

"Yet you uttered a threat against her."

"I did, in my first wrath at the injustice of my sentence; but nearly twenty years of imprisonment removed revenge from my heart I came down to Kirkstone Hall not to kill her, but to implore her to tell the truth, and free me from undeserved shame. But she had fled, thinking in her guilty mind that I intended to harm her. I told Miss Wedderburn that I did not, also Ar—I mean Mr. Ferris."

"You can call him Arthur," said Gebb, coolly. "I know that he is your son."

"Is this so?" asked Dean, looking with some surprise at Ferris.

"Yes, father. I told Mr. Gebb the truth, or, rather, I admitted it, as he had already learned my relationship to you from Prain. He knows everything, and we have come to ask you to right yourself in his eyes—to confess."

"Confess, Arthur! Do you believe that I killed Kirkstone?"

"No," said Arthur, with conviction, "I do not."

"And you, Edith," said Dean, looking at the girl, "is it your opinion that I am guilty of Miss Gilmar's death?"

"No," replied Edith, in her turn. "Appearances are against you, but I truly believe you to be guiltless."

"And so I am, for——"

"Before you go on," interrupted Gebb, looking up, "I think it will be best for you to approach this matter with more particularity. Were you not at Grangebury on the night of the twenty-fourth of July?"

"Yes," admitted Dean, promptly, "I was. I went to see Mr. Basson, who had been my counsel."

"About what?"

"About the confession of Miss Gilmar."

"What!" cried Gebb, in surprise. "You found it?"

"I found it on the twentieth of July, concealed in the Yellow Boudoir, where Ellen Gilmar had hidden it. I know now who killed Kirkstone."

"Miss Laura!" cried the detective, knowing Dean's belief.

"No. Miss Gilmar herself was the murderess."

"Well, I never!" said Gebb; and looked at Edith and her lover, who were not much astonished. "And where is the confession now?"

"Mr. Alder has it," was the unexpected reply.

"Alder! Why, he believes you to be guilty. He said so several times."

"I asked him to," replied Dean, quickly; "Mr. Alder has been a good friend to me all through."

"He has been a good friend to us all," said Edith, touching Arthur's hand. "Does Mr. Alder know who you are?"

"Yes. He had been present at my trial, you know, and, in spite of my altered appearance, he recognized me on one of his visits to the Hall. I begged him to keep my secret, and he did. I asked him to talk of me as guilty, so that I might be the more effectually concealed."

"I don't see how that would help you," interrupted Gebb, sharply.

"Why not? If Alder had gone about insisting that I was innocent, you might have suspected that he had seen me lately; while by stating what everybody believed, no questions would be asked."

"True enough," said Gebb, his brow clearing. "But I confess this disjointed information of yours puzzles me not a little. Suppose you tell us the whole story from the time you first masqueraded as Mad Martin."

"Certainly," assented Dean, readily. "I intended to do so, as I wish you to help me to establish my innocence. Also, I owe it to my son and Miss Wedderburn to relate things I formerly kept from them."

"We are all attention," said Edith, and leaned forward eagerly.

"When I was feigning madness at the Hall," said Dean, glancing at his three auditors, "I was wondering all the time how I could prove my innocence of Kirkstone's murder. One night, Mrs. Grix— who had found out my true name—told me that Miss Gilmar had written a confession of the crime; and—as she believed—had hidden it in the house. She gathered this from some words let fall by Miss Gilmar. Thenceforth it became the aim of my life to find that confession; but although I looked everywhere, I could not discover it. Then Mr. Alder came visiting at the Hall, as you know, Edith, and he guessed who I was. Feeling that I could not deceive him, I confessed that I was really Marmaduke Dean, and consulted him as to the possibility of proving my innocence. Alder scoffed at the idea of a confession being in existence, as he said if Miss Gilmar were guilty, she would not put the fact down in black and white. He advised me to consult Basson, who had been my counsel, and to see if I could not be cleared; but this I was afraid to do, lest Basson should hand me over to the police."

"Oh, he would never have done that," said Gebb, remembering the personality of Basson, "he is good nature itself."

"So Alder said," continued Dean. "Still I was too afraid to venture, and remained in hiding at the Hall, thankful that Alder kept my secret I must say that in every way he acted like a true friend, for he could easily have given warning about me to the authorities."

"I wonder he did not do so for Miss Gilmar's sake," said Gebb.

"Had he deemed me guilty he would have done so," cried Dean, quickly; "but I told him the whole facts of the case, and declared that Laura, being possessed of the knife, had killed her brother. Alder in the end said he believed in my innocence, but he declined to look upon Laura as the assassin. He fancied that Miss Gilmar had committed the crime, and to shield herself, and punish me for not being in love with her, she accused me. Still, he declined to believe that she had confessed her guilt in writing. I was certain, however, from what Mrs. Grix said, that she had, and——"

"This is all very well," interrupted Gebb, quickly, "but it does not explain your visit to Grangebury."

CHAPTER XXIV

PROOF POSITIVE

Impatient of the interruption, Dean looked at Gebb in a quick, irritable way, like a man whose nerves are not under control; but, in his own interests, he answered quietly enough—

"I am coming to the Grangebury visit shortly," he said, "but it is necessary for me to explain what led to it, so that you may not misunderstand my reason for going there."

"I beg your pardon, Mr. Dean," replied the detective. "Pray go on."

"As I said before," continued the prisoner, "I was certain that Miss Gilmar had left a confession behind her, and after months of search I found it."

"Where?" asked Edith, much interested.

"In the Yellow Room. It was sewn into the hangings, between the satin and the lining, and, but for the particular minute search I made, would never have been discovered. I dare say Ellen Gilmar hid it thus safely so that she might not be accused of the crime in her lifetime; but no doubt when dying she intended to indicate its hiding-place, so that I might be set free and my character cleared, after she was safe from the punishment of man."

"As she is," observed Ferris, bitterly.

"Leave her to God," said Dean, slowly. "As she has sown, so shall she reap, and I wish her no worse fate. Well," continued he, "you will understand that as soon as I discovered this proof of my innocence I was bent upon clearing myself. But this was not so easy to do. I had escaped from gaol, and were I discovered would be at once taken back, when, as I fancied, the confession might go astray or prove useless. It was towards the end of July last that I found it, and I consulted Mr. Alder, who came down about the same time to visit Edith."

"Yes," said Edith, colouring. "He came to ask me again to marry him."

"Alder advised me to place the confession in the hands of Basson, and offered to take it up to him. But at the moment I was unwilling to let this proof of my innocence leave my hands, and I determined to go up to London myself and see Basson. But, thinking I might be discovered, I feared to do so—or at all events to go to Basson's office. I wrote and told Alder this, so he suggested that I should go to Grangebury, where Mr. Basson was giving a lecture, on the twenty-fourth of July, and he said I could come up late and see Mr. Basson before the lecture, place the confession in his hands with instructions what to do, and then return by a late train to Norminster. Thus, he said in his letter, I should be exposed to less risk of discovery. The advice seemed good to me, and I adopted it."

"But where did you get the money to visit London?" asked Edith. "For I never gave you any."

"I borrowed it from Mrs. Grix, and told her I was visiting a friend," explained Dean. "Also I asked her to tell you that I had gone into Norminster, in case you missed me."

"I didn't miss you at all, and there was no need for Mrs. Grix to say anything," said Miss Wedderburn. "All the same," she added reproachfully, "you might have trusted me."

"And me also," interposed Ferris. "I should have had the confession, not Basson."

"You are right," replied his father, with a sigh. "I behaved foolishly, I admit; but I acted, as I thought, for the best. On the twenty-fourth of July, by the five o'clock train, I went up to Grangebury."

"Did you know that Miss Gilmar was there?" asked Gebb, with a glance at Edith.

"No, I did not," answered Dean. "Why do you ask?"

"Because Miss Wedderburn knew of Miss Gilmar's whereabouts."

"That is true enough," responded Edith, calmly; "but I did not think it necessary at the time to tell Mr. Dean. No one but myself— and later on Arthur—knew that Miss Gilmar was lodging in Paradise Row. Continue, Mr. Dean!"

"I arrived late in Grangebury, about six o'clock, and went to a public-house, where I had some tea, and made myself as respectable as possible to go to the lecture. I intended to see Mr. Basson before it began, and then take the nine o'clock train to Norminster."

"Had you a return ticket?" asked Gebb, remembering the one found in the Yellow Room.

"Yes; a third-class return. However, in the public-house I fell asleep, being worn out with trouble and fatigue. I did not waken until it was nearly nine o'clock, and then went to the Town Hall. Mr. Basson was already on the platform, so I could not speak to him. Yet I was anxious to get back to Norminster on that night, as I did not want Edith to know I had been in London."

"But why?" said Edith. "You must have been aware that you could trust me."

"I wished you to know nothing, my dear, until Basson proved my innocence," replied Dean, sadly. "But I should have trusted you. I see it now. However, I did not go back that night, for I lost my ticket."

"Where did you lose it?" asked Gebb, eagerly, for this was a most important point.

Dean shook his head. "I can't say," he replied. "I saw Mr. Alder at the door of the Town Hall, and told him that I was going back, but gave him the confession, and asked him to show it to Basson. He tried to get me to remain, but I was bent on returning, and knew that the confession was safe in his hands. I ran to the station, but there found I had lost my ticket, where I know not. I had no money to buy another, so I went back to the Town Hall and saw Mr. Alder again about half-past nine o'clock. Then, to my surprise, I saw Edith enter the Hall."

"I had just returned from getting the necklace from Miss Gilmar," explained Edith. "I came up to Grangebury after you did."

"I did not know you were out of Kirkstone Hall," said Dean. "Well, I did not trouble to wonder why you were there; but lest you should see me I kept myself out of sight. I then explained my position to Mr. Alder. He gave me some money, and advised me to stay all night at Grangebury. I was unwilling to do so, but as the last train had left I was forced to stay. I slept in the public-house where I had been before, and left by the early train next morning."

"Did you hear of the murder before you left?"

"No, as I departed early. So you see, Mr. Gebb, I can prove an alibi; for at the time of the murder—ten o'clock it was, the paper said—I was asleep in the public-house. The keeper of it can prove that I was."

"What is the name of the public-house?"

"The Golden Hind, near the railway station."

Gebb noted this name in his pocket-book, and rose to his feet "So this is all you have to tell me?" said he, briskly.

"All!—and enough, too. I don't know who killed Ellen Gilmar. It was not I."

"If the hotel keeper can prove your alibi that will be all right, Mr. Dean. But this confession; you say Mr. Alder has it?"

"Yes. But I asked him to make no use of it," replied Dean, "for, as I was in Grangebury on the very night—about the very hour—that Ellen was murdered, I was afraid, if Alder acted on the confession, I might be accused of the second crime. Certainly I had a defence; but the evidence was so strong against me that I did not wish to risk appearing."

"Do you know who killed Miss Gilmar?"

"No!" cried Dean, vehemently, "I do not."

"Then what about these?" said Gebb, and suddenly produced the jewels of Miss Gilmar. "These ornaments belonged to the dead woman; they were taken off her body by the wretch who killed her. I found them hidden in your room at Kirkstone Hall; yet you swear that you do not know the name of the assassin. What am I to understand by this contradiction?"

"It's a plot to ruin me," said Dean, becoming very pale. "I did not know that these jewels were in my room. I never saw them before. Edith! Arthur! What do you know of this?"

"We know nothing," they said simultaneously.

"Come, Mr. Dean," said Gebb, imperiously, "these ornaments would not have been hidden in your room without your knowledge. If your alibi is to be believed you are innocent, but on this evidence you must know who is guilty."

Dean gave a long sigh, and lapsed into his old sullen manner.

"I know nothing about them," he said in a piteous tone; "some one must have put them there. I don't know who. I have told you the truth, but even that will not help one, and I shall be condemned for the second time—an innocent man. Oh, God is cruel—cruel!" and the tears ran down his cheeks.

After that there was little more to be said. The old man was ill and feeble. For the moment he had braced himself to tell his story, and the hope of being righted had given him unnatural strength; but now that all was told, Nature claimed her own, and Dean fell back on his bed thoroughly exhausted. Ferris desired to stay beside his father, but when the warder came back they would not permit this, and in the end the three left the prison. In the street Gebb turned to speak a few words to Edith before leaving for town, as he had decided to do.

"What are your intentions?" he asked.

"I shall stay here until to-morrow," she replied. "I am too exhausted to return to London to-night But I must go up in the morning, as I promised to see Mr. Alder."

"Alder?" repeated Gebb, who had half forgotten the man; "how is he?"

"Very ill—dying, they say; and he sent for me to see him. I could not go to-day, as I came here with Arthur to see what had been done about his father. Do you think he is innocent?"

"Yes, I do," replied Gebb; "but I am puzzled about the jewels. I cannot help thinking that Dean knows something about them; but he won't speak."

"He may to-morrow morning," said Ferris, quickly. "I think he is too exhausted to-night to remember much more. His memory has been severely taxed to-day, you know. I shall speak to him to-morrow, and whatever he tells me I shall tell you, Mr. Gebb."

"Very well," replied Gebb, dubiously, and walked briskly to the railway station, as he was anxious to reach London, to see Parge and tell him what he had discovered.

Also, he desired the advice of Parge regarding the jewels, for despite Arthur's promise, he did not trust him altogether. The young man had deceived him before, and should occasion arise might do so again. So Gebb determined to act independently of anything which might be said by Dean in the morning. He was surrounded on all sides by people who, with their own ends to gain, were more or less unscrupulous, so it behoved him to be wary. Otherwise, he would never pluck out the heart of this mystery.

On arriving in town Gebb went to his office, and there found three letters for him. Two, from the station-master and the ticket-clerk of Norminster Station, were corroborative of Dean's visit to town on the evening of the twenty-fourth of July; for both stated that Mad Martin, the gardener of Kirkstone Hall, had purchased a return ticket, and had left for London by the five o'clock train. But knowing what he did, this evidence came too late to enlighten Gebb in any degree, so he tossed the letters aside and opened the third one. It proved to be from Parge, requesting him to call and see him at once on important business concerning the Grangebury murder case, these latter words being underlined.

"He has found out something," thought Gebb. "I wonder what it is? another mare's-nest, I expect. However, we'll see. I'll call to-morrow."

At ten o'clock next morning he was in Pimlico, and in the presence of Mr. Parge, who received him with a look of subdued triumph.

"Well, Absalom," said he, "have you discovered who killed Miss Gilmar?"

"No, I haven't, Simon; have you?"

"Yes. I found out the truth from—who do you think?"

"I don't know," said Gebb, impatiently. "Mrs. Presk, perhaps."

"No, not from the mistress, but from the maid—Matilda Crane."

Gebb looked at the ex-detective in amazement. "Why, what did she know about it?"

"She knew who visited Miss Gilmar on the night of the murder. I said you had not examined that girl properly, Absalom, so I sent for her to put a few questions myself. Then I discovered that she had found, cast into the grate among other papers, a letter written by the assassin to Miss Gilmar. Here it is."

Gebb took the bit of paper handed to him, and read as follows:—

"Dear Miss Gilmar,

"I wish to see you on the evening of the 24th July, between nine and ten o'clock, about some information touching Dean. Get rid of every one in the house at that time, and expect me for certain. It will be better for us to be alone. Burn this.

"Yours truly, "John Alder."

"Alder!" repeated Gebb, in amazement; "Alder!"

"Yes! it was Alder who murdered that wretched woman."

CHAPTER XXV

HOW THE DEED WAS DONE

Gebb quite agreed with Parge, regarding the guilt of Alder; and on looking back over the collective evidence, he wondered that he had not suspected him before. No wonder he had come forward to defend Ferris: for bad as he was, the man had some conscience, and did not wish to see a guiltless person hanged for his crime, even though that person was his rival in love. What Gebb could not understand was, why Alder had been so kind to Dean; and it was to ascertain this, amongst other things, that he left Parge as soon as he was able, and went off to Alder's rooms. The man was dying; and for the clearance of all persons concerned in the matter, it was absolutely necessary that he should make a confession of his guilt, even at the eleventh hour.

"I could tell you much that I have discovered," said Gebb, slipping the incriminating letter into his pocket, "but as Alder is dying there is no time to be lost in getting him to confess."

"I agree with you," replied Parge, promptly. "I knew that he was dying, as I saw an account of his accident in the papers. Get him to confess, and for that purpose take Mr. Basson with you as a witness; then come back to me, and tell me everything. I wish to write out all details concerning this very extraordinary case, and put the report in my collection."

"It certainly merits it," replied Gebb, putting on his hat, "and I dare say this confession will be the most wonderful of all. By the way, why did not the servant give up this letter before?"

"Because she is a cunning, artful little minx!" burst out Parge, in great wrath, "and wished to make money over it. She found it, as I told you, while cleaning out the grate, when the room was stripped by Alder. The letter was torn across, as Miss Gilmar evidently did not think it worth while to adopt Alder's advice and burn it. It was lucky she did not, or her death would have gone unavenged; as it is——"

"As it is, the man will escape the law," interrupted Gebb, "but I dare say he'll be punished somehow. I'm sure he deserves to be. Did Mrs. Presk know of 'Tilda's discovery?"

"No! 'Tilda kept the discovery to herself, and intended to sell her information to the highest bidder. It took me two hours to wring the truth and the letter out of her; but I did in the end, and for the evidence I paid her five pounds."

"I've no doubt Miss Wedderburn will pay you when she comes into the estate."

"What, the five pounds!" exclaimed Parge, wrathfully. "Why, I expect the reward."

"But the reward was to be paid by Alder himself," argued Gebb; "and although it was a blind, you can hardly expect the man to pay for his own detection."

"His next heir must pay it!" said the ex-detective, doggedly.

"Miss Wedderburn is the next heir."

"Then I'll apply to her," cried Parge, "I'm going to be paid for my trouble."

"Seems to me, Simon, I've had all the trouble," said Gebb, dryly. "You've sat in your armchair and done nothing."

"I've found out the truth, if you call that nothing!" retorted Parge, growing red. "I've used my brains, which is more than you have done. There is life in the old dog yet, Absalom!"

"And temper also," rejoined Gebb, who was rather sore about the reward "Eh, Simon? Well! well! We'll argue the matter hereafter. I must go to Alder."

"Don't forget to take Basson!"

"No, I won't. But if you are right about Alder, you are wrong about Dean; he did not kill Kirkstone."

"Then who did?" grunted Parge, rather displeased.

"Miss Gilmar herself!" retorted Gebb, and departed swiftly, leaving to his friend this—to him—indigestible morsel.

Parge raged a trifle after Gebb had gone, as he did not like to be put in the wrong; but when he recollected his triumph in the new murder case, he was quite content to set it against his failure in the old one. So he sat placidly in his armchair, and enjoyed his success, and the prospect of getting two hundred pounds with so little trouble. All of which was satisfactory to his wife also; as it kept Parge in a good temper for one entire day, a state of things which was little less than miraculous in that frequently disturbed household.

In the mean time Gebb, with a desperate fear in his heart that he might be too late, went as quick as a hansom could travel to Basson's rooms. Keeping the cab at the door, he ran up the long staircase so quickly that he arrived at the top with failing breath and beating heart. The perennial legend, "Back in five minutes," was still on the barrister's door, and Gebb on knocking was again greeted by the boy in the small suit. This latter admitted that his master was at home, but stated that he could not be seen.

"'Cos he ain't well," explained Cerberus; "he's had a shock!"

"What kind of a shock? An accident?" asked Gebb.

"No," replied the boy, after some consideration, "not that sort of shock. Quite another kind."

"Well, I'm sorry to disturb Mr. Basson," said Gebb, "but you must take him my card and tell him that I must see him. It's a matter of life and death."

The boy still seemed unwilling, but Gebb thrust the card into his hand, and insisted; so in the end it was taken to Basson. In less than a minute Cerberus returned with the information that his master would see Mr. Gebb at once. With a nod the detective stepped into the dingy inner office, and found Mr. Basson with his arms on the mantelpiece, and his head bent down on them in an attitude of dejection. When he heard the footstep of his visitor—and firm, quick, business-like footsteps they were—he turned slowly, and displayed a very pale face and eyes so red that they looked as though he had been crying.

"What is the matter?" asked Gebb, rather taken aback by this evidence of grief.

"I've had a shock," replied Basson, using the very same words as his small clerk had done.

"Nothing serious, I hope?"

"Serious in one way, not in another. Still, I am glad to see you. If you had not come to me I should have paid you a visit in the course of the day. You have a right to know."

"Know what?" demanded Gebb, beginning to feel uncomfortable; he knew not why.

"That Alder is dead."

"Dead!" Gebb, with a burst of anger unusual in one of his self-control, dashed his hat on the floor. "By——!" he used a strong word, "so he has escaped me after all!"

"What!" cried Basson, leaning forward in the chair he had flung himself into. "You know?"

"I know that Alder killed Miss Gilmar; I heard it this morning. I have the evidence of his own handwriting to prove his guilt. When did you hear of it? How did you hear of it?"

"I heard all about it at eight o'clock this morning, shortly before Alder died."

"Then he confessed his crime?"

"He did. I was sent for at seven o'clock at his particular request, and he told me the whole story. In order to clear any innocent person who might be suspected, I wrote down what he said, and got him to sign it. The doctor and myself were the witnesses, and the confession is locked in my desk yonder. I was coming round to your

139

office later on in order to place it in your hands. How did you find out the truth?"

"It's a long story, Mr. Basson. I'll tell it to you some other time. But I learned that he killed his cousin, and I came here to get you to go with me, and force him to confess."

"He did so voluntarily," said Basson, sadly, "and made what reparation he could for his wickedness. Do you wonder that I received a shock, Mr. Gebb? It was terrible to hear a man I had known so long, whom I had liked so much, confess himself a murderer."

"It is terrible, I grant you," replied Gebb, somewhat moved by the grief of the old Bohemian. "I should never have thought it of him myself, as is proved by the fact that I never suspected him. He seemed a kindly, honest, pleasant gentleman. Perhaps, however, there is the excuse that he did the deed in a fit of rage. From what I have heard of Miss Gilmar she was a woman to irritate an archangel."

Basson shook his head. "There is not even that excuse," he said. "The crime was committed in cold blood. He planned and carried it out in the most ruthless manner."

"But why in Heaven's name did he desire the death of his wretched cousin?"

"Money, Mr. Gebb—money. Alder was desperately hard up—on the verge of bankruptcy; and as his cousin refused to help him, he killed her. To gain her wealth was the motive of the act. Well," added Basson, with a sigh, "he did not enjoy his ill-gotten gains long, for in the midst of his prosperity the hand of God struck him down."

"You have the confession, you say?"

"Here it is!" Basson unlocked the drawer of his desk, and took out a sheet, or, to be precise, several sheets of paper, and handed them to Gebb. The detective turned to the end, saw the three signatures, then slipped the papers into his pocket.

"It will take too long reading this just now," he said apologetically, "and I have much to do. Will you be so kind, Mr. Basson, as to tell me the facts in your own way? I am curious to know how so many people concerned in the case came to be collected in Grangebury on the night of the murder."

"Alder collected them," said Basson, nodding; "he planned the whole affair in a most wonderful manner, so as to throw suspicion of the crime on every one but himself. Had he lived he would have escaped all suspicion."

"I think not," replied Gebb, feeling for the letter he had received from Parge; "his own handwriting would have committed him. This

140

is one of those little accidents which mar the plans of the most accomplished criminals. However, that is neither here nor there. Let me hear the confession."

Basson thought for a moment, then began. "It seems that Miss Wedderburn was not the only person Miss Gilmar wrote to; she corresponded also with Alder about business matters, for, as she had left her property to him by will, she did not think that he would betray her to Dean. As a matter of fact, she was simply putting temptation in the man's way, for Alder was desperately hard up, and was looking forward to the time when he would come into possession of Miss Gilmar's money. However, she did not know that, and kept him advised of her changes of address."

"Did he know that she was in Grangebury?"

"Oh yes; but he did not visit her there, for already he was thinking of getting rid of her by violent means. The difficulty was how to do it without incriminating himself. Then two accidents helped him. The first was that while on a visit to Kirkstone, Edith told him that she was bent on getting the necklace for Arthur Ferris, and was going up to Grangebury on the evening of the twenty-fourth of July to get it. Ferris, she said, was to escort her. Later on, while Alder was still in the hall, Dean told how he had discovered Miss Gilmar's confession, and wished to give it to me. He was afraid, however, to come to my office lest he should be recognized. Afterwards Alder induced me to lecture at Grangebury, and wrote to Dean telling him to come up and see me there. Then he gave Ferris tickets for my lecture, and told him he could wait for Miss Wedderburn in the Town Hall, while she went to see Miss Gilmar. So now you see, Mr. Gebb, that on the twenty-fourth of July Alder had these three people likely to be suspected on the spot."

"A very ingenious idea," said Gebb. "I suppose he didn't care on whom suspicion fell?"

"I don't think he did," admitted Basson, candidly; "but he preferred to be guided by circumstances, and he really wanted the suspicion to fall upon Dean, as he had threatened to kill Miss Gilmar. Well, you know about Arthur and Edith."

"Yes, I know that he waited in the Town Hall, and that she got the necklace and joined him later, and that they both returned to London. Also, I know that Dean came up, and as he was too late to see you, gave the confession to Alder. But I don't know how Alder managed to get away from the hall without suspicion."

"Oh, that was easy," replied Basson. "He was busy seeing after the tickets on my behalf, and looking at the house; so none of the attendants knew where he was at the moment, but believed him to be in another part of the Town Hall. When Edith came back with the necklace he sent her into the hall, and got rid of Dean, who had missed his train, by giving him money and telling him to stay all night in Grangebury—a fact which favoured his plans; then the coast being clear, he went alone to Paradise Row shortly before ten o'clock, and saw Miss Gilmar. In accordance with his instructions she was alone in the house, as she had sent Mrs. Presk and 'Tilda to my lecture."

"She admitted him?"

"Yes, and locked the door after he was inside; but he did not see where she hid the key. He then told her that Dean had found the confession, and Miss Gilmar, as you may guess, was in a great state. She immediately, with her usual superstition, got out the cards, to see what would happen."

"And she turned up the death-card?"

"Yes. How do you know?"

"Because I found it in her lap."

"Yes," said Basson again, "she picked up the death-card, and while gazing at it in horror Alder, who was striding about the room smoking, slipped behind her, and with a cord torn from the nearest curtain, strangled her. He then robbed her of all her jewels and slipped them into his pocket. Then he tried to get out, but found the doors locked, and did not know where the keys were."

"Mrs. Presk had the key of the back door, and Miss Gilmar that of the front," said Gebb.

"Quite so; but Alder did not know that. He did not dare to get out by the window, lest he should be taken for a burglar, and arrested; so he stepped down to the kitchen and waited till Mrs. Presk came home. He heard her go upstairs and then call 'Tilda, so that he knew the crime had been discovered. When the servant went up to the Yellow Boudoir, Alder ran out of the back door, and returned to the Town Hall. The people in charge of the money and tickets thought that he had been with me, I fancied he had been with them, and as no inquiries were made, you see nobody could guess that he had been away and had committed a crime."

"And why did he leave the jewels in Dean's room at Kirkstone Hall?"

"Ah, you know that?" said Basson, much surprised. "Why, he hid them so as to throw the blame on Dean. Everything was suspicious against the man. He was presumably guilty of the first crime, he had threatened to kill Miss Gilmar, he was in Grangebury on the night of the murder, and the jewels—as Alder arranged— were to be found in his room."

"They were found," said Gebb. "I found them, and for the

142

moment believed Dean guilty. But about that ticket found in the Yellow Boudoir?"

"That was purposely dropped there by Alder to further incriminate Dean."

"How did he get the ticket?"

"In giving the confession it fell out of Dean's pocket, and Alder picked it up. So you see, Mr. Gebb, that in every way chance played into Alder's hands."

"'The wicked flourish like a green bay tree'; but not for long," said Gebb, grimly. "But tell me. Why was Alder so kind to Ferris?"

"Oh, that was his deceit," said Basson, with a sigh. "He fancied that when Dean was accused of this second murder Edith would never marry Ferris, as being the son of such a man. He was kind to him because he wanted to ingratiate himself with Edith: so that she might marry him after parting, as he thought she would, with Ferris."

"Infernal scamp!" cried Gebb, swearing, "when he knew that the poor devil was innocent. Have you Miss Gilmar's confession?"

"Here it is; Alder gave it to me. It clears Dean entirely, so I suppose he'll receive a free pardon."

"I suppose so," said Gebb, putting the confession of Miss Gilmar into his pocket along with that of Alder. "But his life is ruined. I'm only sorry for one thing: that Alder did not live to be hanged."

"Well, I cannot agree with you; after all, he was my friend," said Basson, sadly.

"He was a blackguard," retorted Gebb, and took his departure.

CHAPTER XXVI

THE END OF IT ALL

One month after the death of John Alder, the two detectives, Parge and Gebb, sat in the room of the former, discussing the now solved mystery of the Grangebury Murder Case. On the table there lay a cheque for two hundred pounds made payable to Absalom Gebb, and signed by Edith Wedderburn. The conversation was mostly about this cheque and how it should be divided between them so as to compensate each with due fairness. The matter was a delicate one, and could not be settled without some sharp words on either side.

"After all, Simon," remonstrated Gebb, in vexed tones, "I did most of the work and deserve the reward for my pains."

"You don't deserve all of it," retorted Parge, captiously.

"I don't claim all of it. I say divide it into two parts of one hundred pounds each. That will pay me, and much more than compensate you."

"I don't know so much about that," grunted the fat man. "I've done a deal of thinking over the case, I can tell you. And it was me who found out the murderer. So in justice I ought to have the whole two hundred pounds."

Gebb snatched up the cheque, and slipped it into his pocket. "If you talk like that you won't have a single penny!" he cried wrathfully, for he was disgusted with the avarice of his coadjutor. "In the goodness of her heart Miss Wedderburn considered that she should pay the reward out of the estate, and did so—to me; there was no word of you, Mr. Parge, when she signed this cheque."

"I dare say not," growled Simon, savagely, "that's gratitude, that is; yet if it hadn't been for me her father-in-law to be would have swung for a murder as he didn't commit."

"Don't you make any mistake about that, Simon," replied Gebb, dryly, "Mr. Dean could have proved his innocence without you in both cases. The confession of Miss Gilmar shows that she killed Kirkstone, and the evidence of the hotel-keeper of the Golden Hind proves that Dean slept there at the very hour of the murder. He would have been declared innocent even if you hadn't discovered the truth."

"Well, I did, anyhow," declared the other, sulkily.

"So did Mr. Basson, if you come to that."

144

"Rubbish!" cried Parge. "He only heard the confession of Alder."

"Well, and didn't that reveal the truth? As a matter of fact, in the face of that confession, Miss Wedderburn need not have paid the reward to any one. However, she thought that I deserved payment for all my work, so she gave me this money. It is only because you are a pal, and because I know you've helped in the matter, that I give you fifty pounds for yourself."

"Fifty pounds!" roared the fat man, growing purple with rage. "You said one hundred just now."

"So I did; but I've taken off fifty for your greediness, Simon. I don't need to give you a single stiver if it comes to that."

"I'll never help you again!"

"Much I care!" retorted Gebb. "I can get on without you. And I can't say as I care to work with a man as doesn't know when his friend is doing him a good turn. You say another word, Simon Parge, and I'll reduce your reward to twenty-five pounds."

If Parge had been able to move he would no doubt have fallen on Gebb; but chained as he was to his chair, he could do nothing but glare at his junior with a fierce eye and a very red face. He knew very well that Gebb was acting in the most generous manner in offering to share the reward, so, fearful of losing all by opening his mouth too wide, he sulkily signified that half a loaf was better than none.

"I dare say it is," said Gebb, tartly; "but you only get a quarter of a loaf. I brought two fifty-pound notes with me, but as you have been so avaricious, you shall only have one. There it is;" and Gebb clapped a Bank of England note into the hand of Parge, which closed on it readily enough.

"And you keep one hundred and fifty," he said, with a frown.

"I do; and I've earned it, Simon, by the sweat of my brow. But now that I've behaved towards you a deal better than you deserve, I'll go and bank my money. You'll not see me here again in a hurry."

"No, no!" cried Parge, seeing that his greed had carried him too far, and softened by the money, which, after all, had been earned very easily. "Don't go, Absalom. I can't do without you."

"Haven't I been generous, Simon?"

"Yes, you have. Don't take a man up so short. Sit down and have a pipe and a glass of grog, and a talk over the case."

With some dignity Gebb accepted the olive branch thus held out, and resumed his seat. Afterward Parge seemed so repentant of his late behaviour that the dignity of Absalom disappeared altogether; and, moreover, the whisky and tobacco proved strong

145

aids to patching up the quarrel. In ten minutes the pair were chatting together in the most amicable fashion.

"Well, Absalom," said Parge, with a plethoric grunt, "and how does the matter of that Grangebury case stand now? You know I'm shut up here, and never hear a word of what's going on. Tell me the latest news."

"Miss Wedderburn has inherited the Kirkstone property."

"She owns the Hall, then?"

"Yes, she inherits the Hall, and also Miss Gilmar's personal property. It was left to Alder first, and failing him to Miss Wedderburn, so she is now a rich woman, and I dare say will make a better use of her money than the old skinflint who left it to her."

"She'll buy a husband with it, I suppose," said Parge, ill-naturedly.

"Don't you make any mistake," contradicted Gebb, friendly to both Edith and Arthur. "She was engaged to Ferris in the days of her poverty, and she'll not throw him over now that she is rich; but there is no purchase about the matter. I dare say Ferris will yet succeed with his pictures. In the mean time, he is to marry Miss Wedderburn, and good luck to both of them, say I. They are as decent a young couple as I know."

"When docs the marriage take place?"

"Next month. Old Dean can't live long, and he wants to see the pair man and wife before he leaves this very unjust world."

"Unjust world!" echoed Simon, incredulously. "Dean has been pardoned, has he not, Absalom?"

"Of course; pardoned by the State for a crime he never committed, after passing nearly twenty years in gaol for Miss Gilmar's sake. I don't wonder the old fellow is dying. He is worn out with trouble and a sense of harsh injustice. He has one foot in the grave now, and I expect he'll drop into it as soon as his son marries Edith Wedderburn."

"And he didn't kill Kirkstone after all?"

"No," replied Gebb, with something of a dismal air. "It appears from the confession left by Miss Gilmar that she struck the blow. Do you remember the bowie-knife mentioned in the evidence as belonging to Dean?"

"Yes, the knife with which the man was killed," said Parge. "The sister borrowed it from Dean, didn't she?"

"Yes; and it appears that in her rage against Ellen Gilmar for presuming to love Dean, she threatened her upstairs with the knife, while Kirkstone and Dean were quarrelling in the smoking-room. Ellen wrenched the knife away, and said she would take it at once to Dean in the Yellow Room. She went down with it, and found that

146

having quarrelled, Dean and Kirkstone had parted, the former having gone up to bed Ellen entered with the knife in her hand, and laid it on the table. Then Kirkstone, who was in a bad temper, began to insult her. She retorted, and in a short space of time they were at it hard. Then when Miss Gilmar said something unusually cutting to Kirkstone, he rushed at her to strike her. She snatched up the knife to defend herself, and held it point out. In his blind rage he dashed against it, and the point pierced his heart. He fell dead on the spot."

"Oh," said Parge, reflectively, "then it was really an accident!"

"Yes; but Miss Gilmar was so terrified that she hardly knew what to do. Then, remembering that the knife belonged to Dean, and that he had been fighting with Kirkstone, also that he despised her love, she determined to inculpate him, so as to avenge herself and save her own life. She ran upstairs and told him that Kirkstone wished to see him again in the Yellow Room. Dean fell into the snare, and came down only to find Kirkstone dead with the knife in his heart Then he was seized with a panic, and fled back to his room, whence he was dragged when that wicked old woman accused him of the murder!"

"Didn't Dean suspect her?"

"No; he fancied that Laura, to whom he had lent his knife, had struck the blow; but afterwards, when reviewing the circumstances in prison, it occurred to him that Miss Gilmar might be guilty."

"But how did Miss Gilmar quieten Laura?"

"Easily enough! She told her that Dean had taken the knife and had killed Kirkstone. But it seems to me," said Gebb, meditatively, "that if Laura had only given her evidence clearly, the truth about the knife would have been found out."

"I dare say!" rejoined Parge, tartly. "But if you had been in charge of the case, as I was, you would have found out when too late that Laura, being weak-witted and under the thumb of Ellen Gilmar, was afraid to tell the absolute truth."

"Nevertheless, the case was muddled," insisted Gebb.

"Absalom!" cried Parge, fiercely. "You can take the best part of the reward if you choose, but you shan't throw discredit on my past work. I conducted the Kirkstone murder case to the best of my ability."

"And punished the wrong man."

"That was the force of circumstances."

"It was the want of getting the necessary evidence," retorted Gebb, with some heat. "However, we have improved since then in detective matters, as in others."

"Oh, have you?" growled Parge. "Then why did you arrest the wrong man in the person of Ferris?"

"You have me there, Simon, you have me there," laughed Gebb; which admission put Parge into great good-humour.

"And criminals nowadays are just as stupid as they were in my youth," he said, waving his pipe. "For instance, why did Alder kill Miss Gilmar?"

"Because he wanted her money."

"Well, by threatening her with Dean he could have got her to allow him a good income. There was no need for him to strangle her."

"Perhaps not; and especially in poor Mrs. Presk's front parlour. She hasn't been able to let it since. And, to make matters worse, Matilda Crane has gone away with the five pounds you gave her."

"Mrs. Presk had better give up the house at once," said Parge, nodding. "No one will occupy a room in which a murder has taken place. 'Taint nat'ral to live with ghosts. What about that Yellow Boudoir at Kirkstone Hall?"

"Oh! Mr. and Mrs. Ferris are going to pull it down when they come back from their honeymoon, I expect they will build another wing."

"By the way, is Ferris going to stick to that name?"

"Well, no; but all the same he isn't going to call himself Dean."

"Then he is going to take his wife's name, I suppose?" suggested Parge.

Gebb shook his head "By the will of that ancestor who left the Hall to his descendants, all who live in it not being Kirkstones have to take that name. If Alder had lived he would have called himself John Kirkstone."

"Like the one that was murdered. A bad omen!"

"Well, he never had a chance of changing his name. But I expect Ferris and Miss Wedderburn will call themselves Mr. and Mrs. Arthur Kirkstone."

"Well," said Parge, raising his glass, "I hope they will be lucky."

"So do I," responded Gebb, "If only because they paid this two hundred pounds."

"Of which I got only fifty," grumbled Parge, and so got the last word after all.

THE END